HIS VIRGIN ASSISTANT

BILLIONAIRE BOYS CLUB BOOK 2

K.L. RAMSEY

His Virgin Assistant (Billionaire Boys Club Book 2)

Copyright © 2022 by K.L. Ramsey

Cover Design: Taylor Dawn at Sweet 15 Cover Designs

Formatting: Mr. K.L.

Imprint:Independently published

First Print Edition: April 2022

All rights reserved.

No part of this book may be reproduced, scanned, or distributed in any printed or electronic form without permission. Please do not participate in or encourage piracy of copyrighted materials in violation of the author's rights. Thank you for respecting the hard work of this author.

This is a work of fiction. Names, characters, places, and incidents either are the product of the author's imagination or are used fictitiously, and any resemblance to locales, events, business establishments, or actual persons—living or dead—is entirely coincidental.

Welcome to the Billionaire Boys Club where the men are hot, rich, and very bossy. They make being in charge look easy and their custom-made suits look sexy as sin. Confidence is not a problem for these guys—well, not until they find the women that they want and are turned down flat. Sparks will fly, tempers will flare, and there's sure to be a whole lot of steam when these alphas meet their match.

RODRICK

Rodrick McTavish wasn't going to let his older brother set him up. Hell, it was bad enough that he had to ask his brother for a job after he passed the bar but working at one of the largest law firms in town was a bonus. Plus, he'd taken a lot of shit from his older brother growing up. As far as Rod was concerned, Alex owed him more than one. If they were basing it on beatings alone, Alex owed him a few thousand—but he'd only collect the one favor, a job at his older brother's firm.

He didn't need to work. He and Alex were both set up for life from their grandfather's estate, and working wasn't something that either of them had to do, but they both loved the law, and playing golf every day wasn't really his thing. Rod felt as though he had the best of both worlds—more money than he'd ever be able to spend and a profession that made him want to get out of bed every morning and put on his suit. He knew that his grandfather would be proud of both of them for what they had accomplished.

Honestly, he knew that it was his new sister-in-law's idea to set him up with her friend. He hated the idea, really. Rod might be suffering a dry spell right now, but he certainly didn't need his brother's new wife fixing him up. He was happy and working his ass off trying to make a name for himself in his brother's company. He didn't want to rest on his laurels and have everyone think that he got the job only because he was Alex's little brother. He wanted to prove to them all that he had what it took to be a damn good lawyer, and that took time and dedication—neither of which led to a very exciting dating life.

He had foolishly agreed to have one drink with Evie Jones and then, he'd come up with an excuse to get the hell out of that bar before she'd even be able to order dinner. Sure, that made him sound like an asshole, but he didn't really care. He'd make his new sister-in-law happy, and he'd be able to get on with making money and forming relationships with people who really mattered—his clients.

Rod walked into his brother's office for their morning meeting. He hated having to report in to his big brother daily. He felt like his leash was not only tight but short. Sooner or later, he knew that Alex would cut him a break and let him have a little bit of leeway. "Hey, man," Alex said, looking up from his chair behind his desk.

"How are you this morning?" he asked.

"Good," Alex said. "You?" he asked.

"Ready to get the day started. What do you have for me today?" he asked. Alex had slowly started giving him new clients. They were mostly smaller cases involving arbitration between couples before having to go to court. He was specializing in divorce cases, but he only saw one case go to court. His brother said that was because he was a good lawyer and got couples to cooperate and compromise before they took things to the next level, but he was sure that it was because the couples weren't to the point that they wanted to kill each other yet. That helped a whole lot when it came to arbitration.

"I'm giving you four new cases. Two are going to be a bit different than what you're used to," Alex said. "The couples aren't anywhere near ready to talk things out and compromise. You're really going to have your work cut out for you."

"Hell, I might even see the inside of a courtroom for a change," he said.

"Are you still stuck on that?" Alex asked. "I've already told you, little brother, a good lawyer solves the problem without having to go before a judge or jury." Alex always called him, "Little brother" when he thought that Rod had a lesson that he needed to learn.

"Got it," Rod lied. He just wanted to get out of Alex's office and get on with his day. He'd say whatever his big brother needed to hear to do that.

"You ready for your date with Evie tonight?" Alex asked.

"It's more like just drinks," Rod corrected. He just hadn't told Evie that part yet. The woman thought that he was meeting her for dinner, but he didn't want to blow his plan and come right out and tell her that he only wanted drinks and to cut out early. No, it was better that he'd stick to his ruse and pretend that something came up and he had to leave early. He'd apologize profusely and promise to call her to reschedule, but he wouldn't.

"Does she know that it's only drinks?" Alex asked.

Rod shrugged, "No clue, but what she knows and doesn't know isn't my concern," he said.

"Listen, this woman is one of Nova's best friends. She was there for my wife when she was going through one of the worst periods of her life. Don't hurt her, man. If you don't want to go out with her, come up with a reason to cancel, but don't be an ass to her."

Unfortunately, Nova didn't feel the same way about the situation. "Your wife threatened to cut off my balls if I skipped out on this date, man. There is no way that I'm going to bail on Evie. I'll show up, have a drink with her and see how things go." He knew exactly how they were going to go—he'd get an unexpected phone call from his buddy, Luke, and haul ass out of there.

"She's a nice girl," Alex said. "Just don't hurt her, man."

"Right," Rod said. "Don't fuck it up and don't hurt her. Anything else?" he asked.

"Nope," Alex said. He handed Rod the files from his desk and stood. "I've got to cut out for the morning. It's parent's day at Jack's school and he's asked Nova and me to be there."

"That's great, man," Rod said. He knew how important being a stepdad was to his brother. He took his new responsibilities very seriously. "He's a lucky little guy to have you both."

"Thanks, Rod," Alex said. "If anyone needs me, you have my cell number. But don't need me," he ordered.

Rod chuckled, "Right," he agreed. "I'm sure that the ship won't sink while the captain is away. Have fun, man," he said. He walked Alex out to the private elevators and waved as the doors closed on him. When he was alone in the office, he'd often felt like a kid whose parents left him alone for the first time. It made him feel almost giddy like he wanted to jump on the beds and drink from the milk carton—but he didn't have time for that kind of shit. No, he was going to contact his new clients and set up meetings with them. Then, he'd spend the day in boring arbitrations and hopefully have time to run home for a quick shower and change of clothes before he had to head out to meet Evie. He was going to do the exact opposite of what his brother had just ordered him to do. He was going to fuck things up, but he'd try not to hurt her. He never liked to do that to a woman, even if he was being forced to go out with her. He'd never intentionally hurt her.

EVIE

Evie wasn't sure how she had allowed her best friend to talk her into letting her set her up with Alex's brother. Sure, Alex was the perfect man, but the chances of lightning striking twice and his brother being just as good-looking and sweet were close to zero. She had seen Rod at Nova and Alex's wedding and she knew how handsome he was, but he didn't seem to be as good-natured as his older brother. In fact, he seemed a bit standoffish at the wedding and she knew that she wouldn't be interested in spending time with a man like that—good looking or not.

She had never been very good with the whole dating thing. The fact that she was still a virgin at twenty-two screamed that to be true. She hated having to tell guys that she had never had sex. It was like she'd thrown a bucket of cold water on her date after her admission, and there was no coming back from that. Evie didn't have to tell them, but by the third or fourth date, the guy was expecting more than a kiss goodnight and when she put the halt on his plans, they asked her why and she felt the need to tell them the truth. That was usually when her date would find an excuse to leave early and make every promise to call her to reschedule as soon as possible. It was a lie—they never called her again.

Now, she was sitting in a restaurant waiting for Rodrick McTavish to meet her for dinner and she felt like a high schooler again. "Evie Jones," a deep voice asked. She turned around to look at the tall, dark, and extremely handsome man looking down at her. God, he looked so much like his brother, she felt as though she had hit the jackpot. The question now was if he was as sweet as Alex had turned out to be. He treated her best friend, Nova, like a princess and if she was being honest, a part of Evie wanted that too.

"I'm Evie Jones," she said, standing from her seat, holding out her hand. He took it into his own and damn if she didn't want to swoon.

"Good to meet you," he said. "I'm Rod McTavish."

"I figured you were. I noticed the family resemblance," she admitted.

"Yeah," he said. "Alex and I might be a few years apart in age, but we are often mistaken for the other. He likes to point out that he must look incredibly young if people think that he's me. Drives me crazy, really, and he knows it."

She giggled and took her seat again when he held it out for her. "I bet," she said. "Your brother is funny though, most of the time," she said.

"If you say so," he grumbled. "I seem to find him a whole lot less funny than others do."

"I get that," she said. "I have a younger sister and people are always telling me how nice she is and how it must be so great to have her as a sister and I'm usually like, 'Meh,'" she said. "I mean, you never think that your own siblings are as awesome as others do. It doesn't help that she's my mother's favorite either."

Rod chuckled and she loved how the dimples in the side of his cheek popped when he smiled at her. God, he was sexy. "Alex is everyone's favorite, so I know just what you mean."

The waitress stopped by their table and took their drink orders. She reluctantly ordered a glass of white wine when Rod ordered a bourbon neat. She didn't want him to think she was a prude, but she had to hit the pavement tomorrow in search of a new job and she didn't want even a hint of a hangover plaguing her.

"So," she said, "first of all, thanks for meeting with me. I know that Nova can be a bit persistent when she wants to be. I wasn't planning on going out on a date right now, but she insisted."

"Yeah, my new sister-in-law can be a little pushy when she wants her way, but I don't mind. I feel the same way about dating right now. I've just started at my brother's law firm, and I really don't have time for extracurriculars right now. I'm afraid that my life is pretty boring at this point, but it's nice to get out for one night." Ahh, so this was a one-night thing for him. Good to know—but Evie wouldn't be anyone's one-night fling.

"I understand," she lied. She didn't understand why he'd show up for a date that wouldn't lead anywhere. There would be no promise of a second date. No, "I'll call you soon," or anything of the sort. Rod had met with her just to let her know that he wasn't interested and that just plain sucked.

"Oh?" he asked, "how so? What do you do for a living?"

"Well, I'm a paralegal. At least, I was. That's how I met Nova. We both worked at her ex-husband's firm."

"You wouldn't happen to be her spy, would you?" he asked.

"Ahh, so you know about the whole spy thing then?" she asked.

"I helped my brother on her case to get Jack back, and yes, I knew about you spying for her. Your information was very helpful in helping Alex get custody of Jack back."

"I just told her about her ex's illegal activity, Alex, and well, you did the rest as her lawyers," Evie insisted. Honestly, she was just happy to help her best friend get her little boy back. Nova's ex had no interest in being a father.

He held onto their son just to spite Nova and that made him a complete asshole in her book.

"You said that you were a paralegal," he said. "What do you do now?" he asked.

"Well, I'm sort of in-between jobs right now," she admitted. "After what happened at the firm, I was blackballed for helping Nova. I shared documents that went against my NDA and well, that meant an automatic termination of my contract. I've been trying to find something for a few months now."

"Why not apply at Alex's firm?" he asked.

"Because I don't want any favors, you know? I want to get a job on my own merit, not because my best friend's new husband just gave me one," she said. "It's silly, probably."

"Not at all," he said. "I know how it feels to have everyone think that you've only been hired because you're related to the boss. Everyone thinks that Alex gave me the job because I'm his brother, not because I passed the bar and he's looking to expand his firm. He's looking for young, new lawyers to help grow his business. Hell, his own wife works for him as a junior lawyer, but no one questions her being hired because she's sleeping with the boss."

Evie giggled, "I can't imagine anyone saying that about Nova. She worked so hard to pass the bar after they were married. Alex would kill the person who'd dare to say something like that."

Rod chuckled, "You're right, he would. He's very protective of her, and rightly so. She's pretty fantastic."

"She is," Evie agreed. "I love her as if she was my own sister." The waitress brought back their drinks and asked if they were ready to order. Rod looked like he was trying to decide what to do next, and she wondered if he only wanted to do drinks tonight on their date.

"Why not?" he asked. "You have time for dinner, Evie?" he asked. She wanted to point out that was what she had agreed to for their date, but she found herself nodding instead.

"Sure," she agreed.

"Do you mind if I order for us?" he asked.

"Not at all. The menu is in French, and I have no idea what to order," she admitted. He ordered their meals, and she said a little prayer that she wasn't going to end up with a bowlful of snails or something gross.

"You didn't order me snails, right?" she asked, leaning across the table to whisper her question to him.

He threw back his head, barking out his laugh, and she was sure that he was the sexiest man that she'd ever met. "No," he said. "I wouldn't do that to you, Evie—not when I have a proposition for you." Crap, this was the part where he was going to ask her for one night together and she was going to have to explain to him that she was a virgin. That was the very last thing she wanted to do on their first date— even if it ended up being their only date.

"Proposition?" she questioned.

"Yep," he said. "Come work for me. I know that I'm only a junior-level lawyer, but I don't plan on staying where I am forever. I have a detailed plan about growing my clientele and working my way up quickly. I need a paralegal that I can trust to help me out. How about it?" he asked.

"How do you know you can trust me?" she asked, sending him her sly smile.

"Well, you trust me, or you wouldn't have let me order your dinner in French for you. And you were Nova's spy and helped to get her kid back. I think that makes you pretty trustworthy," he said.

Evie sat back and looked him over, trying to decide if she trusted him and his job offer or if she'd be better off continuing her job search. She had been at it for months now, and she had to admit, it was exhausting trying to find a firm she hadn't been blacklisted in for breaking her NDA. Word spread quickly about what she had done to help Nova and Alex with the case and the bigwigs didn't like it. They turned her down at every interview as soon as they saw her name on their schedule. She'd be turned away as soon as she entered the building at most places. One asshole had her brought up to his office to tell her personally why he'd never hire her. Of course, she took his berating with her chin up and when he sent her on her way, she told him to have a good day. Who the hell does stuff like that? She couldn't seem to bring herself to be mean to other people no matter how mean they were in return to her. That's why she had dropped out of law school and only became a paralegal. She didn't think she'd be able to handle the nasty parts of what came with being a lawyer. What did she have to lose by telling him, yes?

"Come on, Evie," he insisted. "I'll make sure that my brother has nothing to do with hiring you. It'll be great," he promised.

She smiled over at him and nodded. "All right," she agreed. "I'll take the job."

"Great," he said, "then this can be a celebratory dinner. When can you start?" he asked.

"Tomorrow morning?" she asked.

He laughed again and Evie wondered what she had said that was so funny. "Um, you are eager, and I love that, Evie, but tomorrow's Saturday."

She sunk back into her chair and rolled her eyes at herself. "Sorry," she mumbled. "When you don't have to report to an office every day, you kind of lose track of what day it is," she admitted.

"I'm sure," he said, "how about starting Monday?" he asked.

"Monday works for me," she agreed.

RODRICK

Rod wasn't sure how he was going to tell not only Nova but his brother that he had hired Evie. He was going to call them on Friday, after his supposed date, but he chickened out as soon as he got home for the evening. He spent the whole weekend hiding out at his penthouse, for fear of running into either Alex or Nova and having to answer a million questions for them. They set him up to date her, not hire her to be his new paralegal. He'd never date his assistant, even if that was how his brother met his new wife. They were happy, but Rod was sure that starting something with Evie wouldn't end so well for either of them.

He got off of the elevator and walked back to his office. When Alex first asked him to join the firm, he agreed thinking that he'd be down with the rest of the lawyers on the seventh floor. But then, Alex went and asked Rod to join him on the top floor that he reserved for himself. Of course, Rod protested, but Alex insisted and when he did shit like that, there was no going back. So, he moved up to the top floor and had his own corner office that most of the junior lawyers on the seventh floor would have killed for.

"Hey," Nova said, standing from behind her desk. "How did it go on your date with Evie?" she asked. Rod knew that his sister-in-law would have already called her best friend and gotten the scoop about their date. He knew that her asking him was a trap, and he didn't plan on falling for it.

He turned around and smirked at her. "You can't tell me that you haven't already called Evie and gotten every last detail," he said.

"I did call Evie and she's been avoiding me, just like you've been avoiding your brother's calls." She was right, he had been avoiding his brother's calls. He had let every one of Alex's calls go directly to voicemail trying to avoid having to tell his brother that he'd hired Evie and wouldn't be dating her.

"So, you haven't talked to her then?" he asked.

"No," she breathed. "How about you give me the scoop and I'll track down my so-called best friend to talk to her later."

"Well, we went out to dinner and had a very nice time," Rod said.

"So, you're going to see her again then, right?" Nova asked.

"Yes, I'm definitely going to see her again," he agreed. He wasn't lying. He planned on seeing her in just minutes when she was supposed to show up for her first day of work.

"That's great," Nova said. "I'm so happy that things worked out for you both. I knew that you two would hit things off."

"Yep—she's great," he agreed. "Now, if you'll excuse me, I have to get back to my office. I've hired a new assistant and I want to be ready for her."

"Assistant?" Nova asked. "You need an assistant?"

"Well, not really," he admitted. "She's more like a paralegal," he said.

"Is she an assistant or a paralegal?" Nova asked. "You do know that there is a difference, right?"

"Of course I do, but I need someone who can do a bit of both job descriptions and I hope that I've found her," he said. "Have a good day, Nova."

"You too, Rod," she said. He didn't bother to look back to see if she was watching him—he could feel Nova's eyes boring holes into his back. She'd figure it out sooner or later. He was guessing sooner since, according to his watch, Evie was due in the office in the next five minutes.

Rod called down to HR to let them know to expect a new hire and got the empty office next to his own ready for Evie to move into. It had the basics—a desk, chair, computer, printer, and even two chairs in front of her desk, for when clients came in. He hoped that it suited her needs, but he'd help her find something else if that was necessary.

"Hey," Evie said from the doorway to her new office.

"Hi," Rod said. "Um, I hope that you're okay with this. I was planning on it being your new office."

"It's perfect," she said. Evie walked in and dumped her bag onto her new desk.

"I've also called HR and you are due to meet with them, on the second floor, in the next hour," Rod said.

"What's going on here?" Nova asked. She was standing in the doorway and Evie's new office was starting to feel smaller and smaller by the second. "Why are you here, Evie?"

"To start my new job," Evie said.

"Wait—she's your new assistant/paralegal?" Nova asked.

"Yes," Evie said. "I'm sorry that I didn't tell you sooner, I've just been so busy."

"Too busy to call your very best friend?" Nova questioned.

"Yes," Evie defended.

"Doing what?" Nova asked.

"She was hanging out with me," Rod said. "We didn't want to tell you, but we hit it off, and well, that's why neither of us answered when you tried calling this weekend."

"I knew it," Nova shouted, pointing between the two of them.

"Yep, you called it," Rod said. He could feel Evie staring him down as if he had lost his mind and he just hoped like hell that she'd play along until Nova went back to her office.

"Well, I'm happy that you finally accepted a job here, Evie. Now, we'll get to see each other whenever we want. I'm so excited," she gushed. Nova rushed into the office and hugged her best friend who looked like she was just trying to figure out what was going on.

"How about you two catch up later?" Rod asked. "I have a lot to talk to Evie about before she heads down to HR to fill out all of their paperwork."

"Right," Nova said. "How about lunch?" she asked. Poor Evie looked at him as if she was trying to tell him that she needed saving.

"Sorry, Nova," Rod said. "We'll be working through lunch today. You'll have to get on her schedule for another day."

"Boy, you're more of a slave driver than your brother," Nova teased. "I'll leave you two alone so that you can get to work."

"Thanks, Nova," Rod said. "For everything." He wrapped his arm around Evie and pulled her into his side, causing her to make the cutest squeaking noise, he almost wanted to laugh. He waited for Nova to get back to her office before he released Evie and crossed the room to shut the door.

"What the hell did you just do?" Evie whisper shouted

at him. "You told her that we're together? How could you do that?"

"I did it because it's the only way that we'll be able to get anything done around here. You see, Nova is determined to put us together. As soon as I walked in here, she practically knocked me over to ask me a couple hundred questions about our date. She won't let this go, Evie. So, we'll have to pretend that we're together for a while to throw her off track."

"Throw her off track?" Evie asked. "You've lost your mind. Evie is my best friend and knows me better than anyone else does. She'll know that I'm lying and then, she'll hate both of us for being deceitful to her. I won't lie to my best friend."

"Okay, then tell her that you don't want to talk about us. Tell her that things are so new, you don't want to jinx it or something corny like that. She'll accept that and we'll have time to figure out our next move. But you and I both know that if we don't pretend to be dating, she'll ruthlessly keep trying to put us together. We won't have a moment's peace. Do you want that while you're learning your new position here?"

"No," she grumbled. "I'd rather not have to deal with Nova trying to set us up anymore—especially now that we're working together. That would be the worst possible scenario. You and I don't need a relationship messing everything up."

"Agreed," Rod said. "So, we'll pretend to be together

for a while and then, we'll start having little arguments over the next few weeks and before you know it, we'll be able to claim that things didn't work out between us and we're breaking up."

"So soon?" she teased.

"You're joking around now, but it's going to feel like an eternity since you refuse to lie to her. She's not going to just sit back and let you keep all the details to yourself forever. Sooner or later, Nova's going to start poking around, and then, we'll have to figure out a plan B."

EVIE

Evie sat at her desk, rethinking everything that had happened to her in the last twenty-four hours. How could she have foolishly agreed to Rod's plan to tell Nova that they were dating? She was an idiot, that's how. All she wanted to do was call a redo of the whole day, but that wasn't possible unless she suddenly found a time machine.

She had spent half her day in HR, filling out their paperwork, and the other half of the day trying to avoid Nova. It sucked that she was going to have to either avoid or lie to her best friend, but what choice did she have? None because Rod left her with no choice and that just plain pissed her off. Now, she was just waiting for the time to tick away so that she could go home and rethink the past twenty-four hours.

"There you are," Nova said. She walked into Evie's

office and sat down in one of the two extra chairs. "I've been looking everywhere for you. How was your first day?" she asked.

"Oh—you know how first days go," Evie said. "I spent most of my day in HR, filling out their mountain of paperwork."

Nova giggled, "Yeah, Alex had me throw out their handbook because he told me that he planned on breaking most of their rules with me, and we did. I'm betting Rod will have the same take on HR's rules."

"Not really," Evie said. "I mean, we're keeping things under wraps. You and Alex are the only ones who know and we're hoping to keep things that way. This thing between us is so new, I don't want it messing up our work relationship. We've agreed to keep work and our personal lives separate." Evie thought back over every word she just said and tried to count up the lies she had just told her best friend. After she got rid of Nova, she was going to march down into Rod's office and punch him in the nuts for putting her through all of this.

"Well, I can keep a secret," Nova promised. "And I'm sure that Alex will be willing to do so too. But sooner or later, people are going to find out," Nova said. Evie wasn't betting on that happening. Before anyone else could find out about her and Rod's supposed relationship, she planned on staging a breakup. It was the only way to end this crazy ruse without too much collateral damage.

"You all right?" Nova asked.

"Of course I am, why?" Evie countered.

"Because you look angry," Nova said.

"Oh, I'm just exhausted," Evie covered. "I think that I'm coming down with one of my migraines," she lied. "If you don't mind, I'm going to find Rod and let him know that I'm going to head home a little early." She stood and gathered her things, not waiting for Nova to answer her.

Nova pulled her in for a quick hug, "Feel better," she said. "I'll call you later to check on how you're doing."

"Thanks," Evie said. She knew exactly how she'd be doing though—she'd still be pissed at her new boss for putting her in this position, and she had a feeling that nothing would change that—well, except maybe a break-up.

NOVA SEARCHED MOST of the top floor for Rod and finally found him in the employee breakroom having a coffee. She plopped down next to him on the sofa and sighed. "What's up?" he asked her.

"I didn't picture you as a break room kind of guy, Rod," she said. "I've looked everywhere for you."

"Well, you found me," he said. "So, what's up?"

"I'm leaving early," she said. "I have a headache."

"Do you need for me to drive you back to your place?" he asked.

"No," she said. "I just need to get out of here before

Nova finds me again and asks me questions that I can only answer by lying to her."

"Shit," Rod growled. "What happened?"

"My best friend is so happy for us, she had to let me know. How do I respond to her questions? How do I look her dead in the eyes and lie to her? I hate the position that you put me in, Rod," she insisted.

"Hey, I didn't come up with the plan for the two of us to go on a blind date together. That was all Nova's doing. She's the one who pushed us together and honestly, if we have to lie to her to keep the peace around here, I say that falls on her shoulders, not mine." A part of her knew that Rod was right, it still sucked that she had to lie to Nova, and blaming him was easy since he was the one who came up with the plan.

"I just don't think that I can stick with plan A anymore," she said. "What's plan B?" she asked.

"Hell, Evie," he said, "I don't have a plan B. I barely had a plan A. I'm winging it here," he said.

"Great, so we're both screwed," she mumbled.

"How about you go out to dinner with me and we can talk about all of this—maybe even come up with a new plan," he offered.

"No," she quickly said. "Going out to dinner with you is how we ended up here in the first place. Besides, I already have dinner plans," she said. She had planned to have dinner with one of her old college friends tonight. Evie was supposed to meet Tyler at six at the same place she and Rod had dinner, and she had to admit, she was looking forward to seeing him.

"You have a date?" he asked.

She wouldn't call it a date, but there was no way she'd let Rod off the hook that easily. She liked the way her "date" made him squirm a bit. "Yes," she lied. "I have a date."

"Well, you rebounded quickly from your whole stance on dating," he accused.

"What does that mean?" she asked.

"It means, when you and I went out just three days ago, you told me that you weren't interested in dating. It was the one thing we had in common," he said.

"I wouldn't say it like that," she said. "We had other things in common, Rod."

"Not the point, honey," he said. "You said that you didn't want to date because you were going to concentrate on your job search," he reminded. She did say that.

"Sure, but now I have a job," she said. "So, problem solved, and I have a date," she lied again.

Rod stood and took his coffee mug over to the sink, rinsed it out, and put it into the dishwasher. "Doesn't matter to me, really," he lied. She could tell that her having a date was pissing him off, for some reason, and she took some sick satisfaction in knowing that. "I'm just saying that you move fast for a woman who didn't want a date just days ago."

Evie stood, "While I'd love to stick around and discuss

how fast I am with you, Rod, I do have to get home. I'll need to take some medication for my intensifying headache, and then get ready for my date. I'll see you in the morning," she said. She walked out of the breakroom before he could say anything else to her. She knew that Rod would argue with her until she confessed that her dinner plans weren't a date, and that was the last thing that she wanted to do. Let him believe what he wanted to about her—she really didn't care anymore.

TYLER MET Evie at the restaurant, and she had to admit—seeing his smiling face standing at the front entrance was a welcome sight. "Hey, you," he said, pulling her in for a hug.

"I've missed your hugs," she breathed against his neck. "You smell good too."

"Thanks," he said. "I borrowed some of Doug's cologne. I love smelling like my man when I'm not with him. It makes me want to hurry home to him."

"You know, Doug could have joined us tonight," she offered.

"Not on your life," Tyler said. "He said that when the two of us get together, we cackle like hens and while he loves both of us, it's annoying." She giggled, knowing that was true. They were kind of awful when they were together. "He sends his love though."

"Well, send it right back to him when you get home tonight," she said. "I miss him. I think the last time the three of us were together was your wedding." It was a beautiful wedding, and she was lucky enough to be Tyler's "Best woman" for the ceremony. She loved being a part of his special day, but now that her two very best friends were married, she longed for something she never thought she wanted. Watching first Tyler, and then Nova, tie the knot with the person of their dreams made her want the same. She'd just need to find the person first and her dating track record wasn't the best.

They walked into the restaurant and were quickly seated in the back corner, adjacent to where she and Rod sat just days earlier. Seeing their table made her feel the same butterflies that she had when she met him there for their "date."

"You all right?" Tyler asked as if picking up on her mood change.

"Yeah," she said. "I was just here on a date a few days ago and well, we sat there," she said, nodding to the table across the aisle.

"I take it that the date didn't go very well, judging by your sour expression," Tyler said.

"It wasn't that bad," she insisted. "I mean, it did end with me getting a pretty great job out of it," she said.

"You got a new job?" he asked. "That's great. It's been a few months now, right."

"Yes," she said. "I was beginning to worry, honestly, but

then, I went out with Rod and he offered me a paralegal position. I couldn't say no."

"So, you didn't say no to the job, but what about the guy?" Tyler asked.

"Well, that's a complicated story," she said.

"I'm yours for the whole night, Evie," he assured.

"Nova set us up," she said. "Rod is her new husband's younger brother. He works at Alex's firm, and you know how pushy Nova is, right?" She asked.

"Um, yeah," he said. "Nova's the reason why I have a sexy ass husband waiting for me at home." She knew that Nova had set up Tyler and Doug. She had just selectively chosen to forget that part when Nova was insisting that she go out with Rod McTavish.

"We went out last Friday and he admitted that he wasn't doing a whole lot of dating right now because he's concentrating on building his career at Alex's firm. I told him that I wasn't really interested in dating either, you know because I was job hunting. He'd heard what I did to help Nova and Alex get Jack back, and he offered me a job on the spot."

"So, you gave up the chance of dating the hunky McTavish brother for a job?" he asked.

"I didn't give up anything," she insisted. "Rod made it very clear that he wasn't interested in dating anyone right now, and I wasn't about to sit there and spill my guts, telling him that I'm looking for Mr. Right."

"You're still looking for him then?" Tyler asked.

"Yeah," she admitted. "I mean, things definitely slowed down while I was searching for a job, but I'm still looking for the right man. I'll just have to find someone who can get past my little problem."

Tyler grabbed her hand from across the table and held it under his own. "Evie, being a virgin isn't a problem. And if it turns out to be a problem for your date, then, he's not your Mr. Right."

"I know that, Tyler," she admitted. "I'm just worried that I'll never find a man who thinks that me being a virgin is a good thing." Tyler's eyes looked at something behind her and when she heard a man clear his throat, letting her know that they weren't alone, she wanted to hide under the table.

"Please tell me that Rod isn't standing behind me," she mock whispered to Tyler.

"Well, the guy behind you looks a lot like Alex McTavish, but I don't want to make assumptions," Tyler said.

"Hi," Rod said, stepping from behind her. She groaned and sunk into her seat as low as she could go, trying to avoid making eye contact with Rod. She was sure that he had overheard what she had just said about being a virgin to Tyler. The question now was would she be able to live through the humiliation and come back from it?

"I'm Rod McTavish," he said. She could feel her cheeks burning with embarrassment as he held his hand out to Tyler. "Sorry to interrupt your date."

"I'm Tyler Anderson, one of Evie's best friends from college. She, Nova, and I go way back. And this isn't a date-date," he said. "My husband doesn't allow me to date," he teased.

"I see," Rod said. She could feel him staring her down. "Sorry, I was made to believe that Evie had a date tonight," he said. "I guess that I was mistaken."

"It's good to finally meet you, Rod," Tyler said. "We ran into each other at Alex and Nova's wedding, but I didn't get the chance to introduce myself that night. It was a beautiful affair though." Evie agreed, Nova's wedding was gorgeous. It was held in Alex's house, in the ballroom that his grandfather had thrown so many beautiful parties in. Her best friend's wedding had a certain old-world charm, and even though she hadn't met Rod at the affair, she had noticed him. He had shown up stag and every woman in the place had their eye on him.

"Yes," Rod agreed, "that was quite a night. And I got a fantastic new sister from it. Nova is really good for my brother, even if she is a bit pushy with her new brother-in-law."

Tyler laughed, "You have no idea how pushy Nova can be when she wants something. If she wants the two of you together, she'll find a way to make it happen. Might as well just reside yourselves to being together now."

Evie groaned again. "Now, you're just trying to piss me off, Tyler," she said. "You see, I didn't get to the point where Rod lied to Nova and told her that I not only work for him now, but we're also together."

Tyler gasped, "You didn't," he said.

"Oh, he did," Evie hummed. "Now, I have to lie to Nova and pretend to be in a relationship with him," she said, pointing to Rod.

"Him has a name and feelings," Rod insisted. "Besides, pretending to be involved with you is no picnic, honey."

"Perfect," she said. "I say we count this as our first official spat, it's just a shame that Nova isn't here to witness it. How about we save the rest for when we're at the office tomorrow and really give her the full effect."

"Is that your plan?" Tyler asked. "To pretend to break up so that Nova will leave you alone?"

"Pretty much," Rod said.

"That's as far as we've gotten with plan A," Evie said.

"Honestly, this is a shit storm and Nova will see right through it, Evie," Tyler said. "She knows you better than anyone and she'll see right through this little ruse" Evie knew that he was right. If Nova thought that she was lying about being with Rod, she'd call her on her shit, and then, neither of them would ever hear the end of it.

She looked over at Rod who was staring her down. "Why are you even here, Rod?" she asked. "Are you following me?"

"What? No," Rod said. "I came here to get a bite to eat. I had no idea that you'd bring Tyler to the same place that we had our first date."

"For your information, Tyler was the one who suggested this place and that was our only date, Rodrick. Saying that it was our first implies that there will be a second, and there won't be."

Tyler smirked over at her, Rod sitting next to him with the same look on his handsome face, and she wanted to slap both of them. "You two are asses," she said. "I'm not going to sit here and let you both make fun of me."

"How are we making fun of you?" Tyler asked.

"I can see it in your eyes, you're laughing at me," Evie insisted. "And I don't have to sit here and take it. I'll see you in the morning," she said to Rod. "And I'll see you at our Saturday game night. Remember, don't tell Nova anything about our plan," she reminded.

"Jesus, Evie," Tyler said. "You know I hate keeping secrets. I wish the two of you never told me any of this. And you can't show up at my house alone, Nova will know that something's up. If he's not with you for our couple's game night, she'll wonder why."

"I always show up alone to them," Evie reminded.

"Right, but now, Nova believes that you have a partner to bring. She'll wonder why he's not there," Tyler insisted.

"He's right," Rod agreed.

"We'll just have to break up before Saturday then," she said. "Game night is the one time a month that I look forward to going out. I won't have to worry about lying to my friend on my favorite night of the month."

"First, that's kind of sad," Rod said. "And second, we

can't break up in less than a week of being together. Nova will know that we're lying." It sounded to her that no matter what they did, Nova would figure out that they were lying, and with no end in sight, and no plan B, Evie worried that there wouldn't be any way out of this.

"I can't do this right now," she breathed. "I'm sorry to leave before we eat, but I just need to go home Tyler," she said. "Raincheck?"

"Of course," he agreed. "I'll grab some take-out and bring some home to Doug. He loves this place." Tyler stood and pulled her in for a hug, "Talk soon," he promised.

"Absolutely," she agreed, turning back to Rod. "Good night, Rod," she coldly said. He nodded and she turned to leave. She should have stuck with her original plan and just gone home early with a headache but canceling on Tyler wasn't something she wanted to do. Now, she really did have a headache and all she wanted to do was take some pain reliever and slip into her comfy bed. Tomorrow would come soon enough and then; she'd have to deal with Rod all over again.

RODRICK

Rod totally lied to Evie when she asked him if he had followed her. He hadn't found her by chance. He followed her from the office and sat outside of her apartment, trying to get up the nerve to go up to her place and demand the truth from her. He didn't believe for one minute that she had a date tonight and he was about to march up to her apartment and tell her just that when she reappeared from her building and got into her car.

He followed her all the way across town, to the same restaurant that he'd taken her to just days earlier. Rod's heart sank when he saw her hug and kiss the tall, handsome guy waiting for her at the front door to the restaurant. He looked familiar, but Rod couldn't quite place him. He felt like an idiot for not remembering the guy from his brother's wedding. Maybe if he had remembered Tyler, he wouldn't have run into that restaurant and made a complete fool of himself, but it was too late to take that back. He followed Evie in and when he just couldn't take it anymore, he pretended to be there to eat dinner and happened to stumble across her and her date. What he didn't plan on was the relief he felt when he found out that she was having dinner with an old friend from college.

Tyler seemed like a great guy. He ordered two meals for takeout and Rod ordered dinner for himself and then offered to buy him a drink while they waited for their meals to be ready. Tyler took him up on his offer and then things got awkwardly quiet.

"So, you knew Nova and Evie in college then?" Rod asked, trying to make small talk.

"Yes," Tyler said. "We were all roommates for our last two years. We rented this awful little place just off campus, but it was the best two years of my life, you know?" Rod had no idea since the last roommate he had was his brother and they were both minors and had no choice about where they lived. It was one of the reasons why he never really got into a long-term relationship. The commitment of living with someone terrified him. Hell, a woman spending the night at his place terrified him.

"You like her, don't you?" Tyler asked.

"Nova?" Rod asked, playing dumb. He knew what Tyler was asking him, he just wasn't sure that he was ready to give the guy a straight answer.

Tyler threw back his head and laughed, and he knew

that he wasn't going to get away with playing the simpleton. "You and I both know that I was asking if you like Evie, Rod," Tyler insisted.

"You really want to know the answer to that question?" Rod asked.

Tyler nodded, "I wouldn't have asked it if I didn't," he said. "So—you like Evie?"

Rod sighed, "I do," he said. "I didn't want to. Hell, when I showed up here a few days ago, to go on the blind date that Nova set us up on, I was going to offer her one drink and then have my friend Luke call me to tell me that there was an emergency at the office, and I had to go back into work. Luke's the head of security at Alex's firm, and I thought that it was the perfect excuse. I'd tell my sister-in-law that I tried, but that Evie just wasn't the girl for me. But then, we started talking and she was charming and sweet, you know? We ordered dinner and I had a really good time."

"That's a good thing, right?" Tyler asked.

"You would think, but then I put my foot in it and asked her to come work for me," Rod said.

"Why is that a bad thing?" Tyler questioned.

"Because now, I can't like her," Rod said. "I can't work with her and like her at the same time. When Nova started questioning me, I panicked and told her that we hit it off and that we were together. The lies just kept growing from there and before I knew it, I couldn't turn the train around and go back. I was stuck and I trapped Evie with me, not thinking about the fact that she wouldn't be okay with lying to her best friend. She's too nice for someone like me."

"This is very true," Tyler said. "Evie is too nice for any of us. She hasn't had it very easy when it comes to dating. Once she tells the guy that she's a virgin, he bolts, as if there's something wrong with her."

"So, it's true then?" Rod asked. "She's really a virgin?" He wondered how a woman who looked like Evie had gotten through college without losing her virginity.

"Yeah," Tyler said. "I guess she never found the right guy to have sex with. She's very particular, but who can blame her. I've run through some real assholes trying to find my Mr. Right. I was lucky that Nova put Doug and me together. My husband is the best guy I know. I just hope that someday, Evie can find the same kind of guy and live happily ever after like Nova, and I have found. But if you can't be that guy for her, Rod, don't pursue her. Evie deserves the best."

"Understood," he agreed. "I'd never do anything to hurt her, man."

"Good," Tyler said. "I wouldn't want to have to kick your ass, Rod."

"Believe me, that's the last thing I want to happen, Tyler," Rod agreed, looking him over. "You're a good friend. Evie and Nova are both lucky to have you in their lives."

"Thanks for saying that," Tyler said. Their food was delivered to the table and Rod insisted on paying for everything since he had interrupted Tyler and Evie's dinner. "It was good to talk to you, Rod," Tyler said.

"Thanks, you too, Tyler," he said.

"Hey," Tyler shouted, stopping him from walking out the door. "How about you come over to game night on Saturday? I'd love to hang out with you some more and for you to meet my husband."

"Um, do you think that's a good idea?" Rod asked.

"Well, you'll know everyone there," Tyler said. "How about it?"

"Are you trying to piss Evie off?" Rod questioned. "Because if so, I'm in." The thought of showing up and being a part of Evie's weekend plans had him feeling a bit giddy and a whole lot naughty. He just had to be careful not to tell her that he was invited because he knew for certain that she wouldn't show up if she knew.

"Great," Tyler said. "Give me your phone," he ordered. Rod pulled his cellphone from his pocket and handed it over to the guy. He watched as Tyler put his phone number into his phone.

"Text me tomorrow and I'll send you the address," he offered.

"Okay," Rod said, taking back his phone. "What can I bring?"

"We just do munchies and drinks. Bring whatever you'd like," Tyler said. Rod nodded and watched as his new friend left the restaurant. He shoved his cellphone back into his pocket and thanked the hostess on his way out to his car. Yeah—him showing up at game night might not be his best idea, but he liked the thought of keeping Evie on her toes. He had a feeling that not much surprised her, but he was looking forward to being one of the first to do so.

ALEX WALKED into his office and sat down in front of his desk. "Hey, what's up, Alex?" Rod asked.

"Well, I've just been on the phone with a mutual friend, and I've been let in on a little secret," he said.

"Mutual friend?" Rod asked.

"Yep—Tyler," Alex said. Rod suddenly felt a little bit sick.

"Oh, he's a great guy," Rod said.

"Yeah," Alex said. "He told me he invited you to game night. I asked him why he had to invite you and why you wouldn't just come with Evie." Shit—this was what he had worried about. He wouldn't lie to his brother; it just wasn't in him.

"Yeah, about that," Rod said. "I might have told a little white lie to Nova about Evie and me being together" he admitted. "I just didn't want her to try to keep putting us together since Evie works for me now, so I came up with the plan to lie to Nova and dragged Evie into it with me."

"What the fuck, man?" Alex asked. "I can't believe that you lied to my wife like that. You know that I won't lie to her, right?"

"I know, and I wouldn't ask you to," Rod said.

"I'm guessing that you won't be at game night then?" Alex asked.

"Why wouldn't I come to game night? Tyler asked me to be there, and I think that it sounds like fun."

"Bullshit," Alex shouted. "You want to be there to make Evie squirm. You like her, don't you?" he asked. They had been working together for five days now and he had to admit, the more time he spent with her, the more he liked her.

"I do," Rod admitted. "But it's not as easy as me just liking her." He wasn't about to tell his brother that Evie was a twenty-two-year-old virgin. That wasn't his business.

"Right, she'd have to like you back and from the angry scowl she wears around you, I'm guessing that she doesn't feel the same way about you as you feel about her," Alex assessed.

"Shut up, man," Rod grumbled. "I don't know what to do. This all started as a way to get Nova off of our backs. If she didn't push us into the blind date, we wouldn't have to lie to her."

"Wait—you're not blaming my wife for your lies, are you? Because that's probably the dumbest thing I've ever heard. I'm pretty sure that once Nova finds out that you weren't truthful with her, she'll kick your ass," Alex warned.

"I figured," Rod said. "But I can't go back and change things now. Listen, do me a favor, don't tell Nova unless she asks." Alex looked like he wanted to protest, and Rod help up his hands. "I'm not asking you to lie. I'd never ask you to lie to your wife for me but give me some time to figure this all out. I need to figure out how I feel about Evie, and I won't get that chance if Nova finds out about our lie. If Evie feels like she's off the hook, she won't give me a chance."

"So, lie by omission?" Alex asked.

"If you need to label it, sure, but just don't tell her about it, unless she outright asks," Rod said.

Alex ran his hand down his face and groaned. "I really hate this shit, man," he growled. "But if it means that you might end up with Evie, then I promise to keep your little deception to myself—unless Nova flat out asks me about it."

"Thanks, Alex," Rod said. "I appreciate you doing this for me."

"So, we'll see you on game night then?" Alex asked.

"Yep, I'll be there," Rod said.

"What happens if Evie doesn't want you there?" Alex asked.

"Well, Tyler was the one who invited me, and it would be rude to tell him no. I'm betting that even if Evie doesn't want me there, she won't say anything. She wouldn't chance Nova finding out about our lie and she'd never make Tyler feel bad about inviting me. She's sweet like that, you know?" Rod thought that she was the nicest person that he had ever met. He was beginning to look forward to going into work every morning, just so he'd be able to see her beautiful face behind her desk.

"She is," Alex agreed. "She's also very innocent. Don't hurt her, Rod." He knew exactly how innocent Evie was and that was part of the reason why he didn't just ask her out again. He knew that if he did—if he admitted to having feelings for her, things could progress, and then what? Could he take her virginity? He had never been with a virgin in his life, not even when he was one. And if he was able to get past her being a virgin, and they had sex, what would happen afterward? He wasn't sure if he wanted a relationship and that wouldn't be fair to her. Evie deserved better from him. Hell, she deserved better than him, but he just wasn't ready to tell her that yet. Instead, he needed for their charade to continue until he could figure his shit out. Then, he'd decide what to do about Evie and her whole virginity issue.

EVIE

Evie had slept in late that Saturday morning and loved being able to lay in bed until her cat insisted that she get her ass out of bed to feed him. Toby was a real jerk when he was hungry, but she couldn't blame him. It was almost eight in the morning when she rolled out of bed to give him his breakfast.

While Toby ate his kibble, she brewed herself some coffee and sat at her kitchen table. She was excited about game night, but more than that, she was excited to see Tyler and Doug's new place. They had bought their first house together just after Nova and Alex's wedding, but she hadn't had a chance to run over to see it yet.

Evie spent the rest of the day vegging in front of the television, watching sappy rom-con movies, and eating popcorn and ice cream until it was time for her to get ready for game night. She decided to go with a casual look tonight and donned her favorite jeans and sweater. Tyler would never let her live it down if she showed up in sweatpants again. She had made that mistake last month and she'd never do that again. They were merciless with their teasing.

Evie checked her reflection and decided that it was as good as it was going to get, grabbing her keys and purse, slipping on her shoes, she opened her front door and walked right into Rod, his hand up ready to knock.

"What are you doing here?" she asked.

"We need to talk," he breathed.

"Well, have you finally come to break up with me?" She had been trying to get him to break up with her at work for two days now. He had insisted that it was too early in their fake relationship to start fighting and eventually, break up, but she disagreed. The longer they let this disaster go on, the more chance that they'd blow their cover and Nova would find out. She wanted to stop lying to her friend, but more than that, she wanted this tension between her and Rod to dissipate. She was tired of arguing with him. Evie actually like the guy and she had a feeling that they could become friends if they could just get past having to lie to everyone about being together.

"No," he said. "But Alex knows."

"What?" Evie asked. She was about to invite him in to have their conversation but decided against it when he blurted out what he'd come to talk to her about.

"I didn't tell him—Tyler kind of did," he said.

"Tyler kind of did? How is that possible?" she asked.

"It's a long story," he said.

"Well, I'm about to go to Tyler's for game night, so give me the abbreviated version of the story," Evie insisted.

"Tyler invited me to game night," he said.

"When did he do that?" Evie asked.

"After you left him stranded for dinner, we both got takeout and he let me buy him a drink. That's when he asked me to attend," Rod said. "Just a reminder—you were the one who told Tyler about our little lie."

"Right, I remember," she assured.

"Well, Tyler apparently told Alex that he invited me to game night and Alex showed up in my office asking why Tyler had to invite me and why I wasn't just coming with you."

"And you told him about us lying to Nova," she said.

"No, he guessed that we weren't being completely honest with them, and I can't lie to my brother," he said.

"While I find that admirable, Rod, I've been lying to a woman who I consider a sister for almost a week now, and you didn't think twice about asking me to do that. I can't believe this. You are such a hypocrite," she shouted, "we're telling Nova tonight. I'm done with this stupid game."

"This isn't a game, Evie," Rod said. "I honestly thought that I was doing the right thing. I'm sorry."

She pushed her way out of the door and locked it behind her, just about shoving him out of the way. "Let's go," she said, grabbing his hand. She pulled him along to his

SUV and jumped into the passenger side. He slipped into the driver's side and looked her over.

"What the hell are you doing?" he asked.

"I'm making sure that you don't back out of this. We're going to Tyler's for game night, and you are going to tell Nova everything—including the part where this whole thing was your idea and that I was against lying to her from the start," Evie said.

"You honestly don't trust me to show up at Tyler's?" he asked.

"Nope," she said. "I think that you'll find a way to get out of it. If I go with you, then you won't have the chance to back out on me."

"Won't showing up together look like we're actually together?" he asked.

She shrugged, "I don't care, really. We'll just sit Nova down and tell her that you made the whole thing up."

"And then what? We sit around and play board games like nothing happened?" he asked.

"Well, that's what I plan on doing. You are welcome to leave if you don't want to stick around," she insisted.

"I don't think that you've thought this through, honey," he drawled. He turned onto Main Street, and she knew that they were almost to Tyler and Doug's. "If I leave you at Tyler's place, you won't be able to get home since I'm your ride." Shit—he was right.

"I'm sure that Nova and Alex will give me a ride home," she countered.

"Sure, after we spill our guts to Nova, she's going to be kind enough to run you home after game night." She knew that he was right about that too, and she wanted to tell him to just shut up. She hated that he was right. Hell, she hated this whole situation.

"What would you have us do then?" she asked. "I mean, you obviously don't want to come clean with Nova, even though it's only a matter of time before her husband tells her. Tyler can't keep a secret to save his life. If he's already hinted to Alex what's going on, he'll do the same with Nova. Then what will we do? Telling her ourselves before anyone else does is the only way."

"No," Rod said, "it's not the only way, honey. We could actually not lie to her another way." She was trying to keep up with him, but Rod wasn't making much sense.

"I'm not following," Evie admitted.

"If we were really together, then we wouldn't be lying to anyone," Rod said.

"You can't be serious," she said. "You and me?" she asked.

"Sure," he agreed. "Why not?"

"Because we can't have one conversation with each other without it ending in a fight," she said. "Plus, you know my situation, Rod, and don't pretend you don't. I know you overheard Alex and me talking about my um, status," she said. God, she usually had no problem telling a guy that she was a virgin. Why was it so hard to say that word to Rod?

"You mean, the fact that you're a virgin?" he asked. He parked in front of Tyler's new place and turned off the engine. She couldn't look at him, but she knew Rod was staring her down as if daring her to give him the words.

"Yes," she breathed. "I'm a virgin. I'm betting that you don't date many of those, Rod." He pulled her hand into his own and she still couldn't look at him.

"Evie," he whispered, "look at me, please."

"I can't," she croaked.

"Please," he said again.

She was never one to cower at one of his demands but looking at him and having this conversation wasn't something that she wanted to do. Still, she found herself turning to face him. Rod leaned in and gently kissed her lips.

"What are you doing?" she stuttered, breaking their kiss.

"I'm just seeing something," he said.

"Seeing something?" she asked.

"Yeah, be quiet and let me figure this out," he ordered. He smiled and pulled her in for another kiss, this time, she didn't pull away or want him to stop. If he was seeing that they were compatible, she'd give him his answer—they were.

"Wow," Rod breathed. "Tell me you didn't feel that," he said.

"Do you mean that spark?" she asked. She felt it but telling him that might not be her best idea. What option did she have—he'd just keep kissing her until she admitted that she felt the same thing as him.

"I felt it," she admitted. "The sparks, I mean."

"Thank fuck," he growled.

"It doesn't change anything," Evie insisted. "We still lied to Nova and she's still going to find out."

He cupped her jaw in his big hand and she couldn't stop herself from leaning into his touch. "Just give this a chance, honey," he said. "Please."

She shouldn't have agreed to it, really. Evie should have told him that she wasn't going to jump into a relationship with him just so she could claim not to be lying to her best friend, but she wanted what he was offering. She found herself nodding her agreement to his plea, and before she knew it, she was practically on his lap. Rod pulled her across the center console and wrapped her in his arms.

"Thank you, honey," he said.

"We still have a lot to talk about, Rod," she warned. "But Nova and Alex just pulled up and now isn't the time."

She watched as her best friend got out of Alex's car, smiling ear to ear, walking to Rod's SUV. "We need to go in," Evie said.

"All right but promise me that when we get back to your place, you'll ask me in so that we can talk," he said.

"Talk," she asked, "just talk?"

"Sure," he agreed, "unless you have a better idea." She could come up with about a thousand other things she'd like to do than just talk, but they weren't ready for that next step. Technically, they had only been together for a matter of minutes now, so talking was going to have to be enough.

"Just talking," she grumbled. Rod chuckled and helped her out of his SUV.

"You guys beat us here," Nova said, pulling her in for a hug. "I'm so excited that we're all here tonight." She released Evie and tugged Rod down for a quick hug. Evie noted the way Alex looked between the two of them with a knowing smirk on his face.

"How's it going?" Alex asked his brother.

"Great," Rod insisted. "Ready for game night."

"What did you bring?" Evie asked Nova nodding to the casserole dish.

"Well, I made some mac-n-cheese. I've been craving it like crazy." She smiled up at Alex and he took the dish from her. Evie wondered why Nova had stressed the word, "Craving" the way she had, and then it all seemed to click.

"Wait," Evie said, "are you pregnant?" she asked.

Nova smiled and nodded, her eyes welling with tears. "I am," she croaked. "I just found out and we're not really telling many people—just you guys and Tyler and Doug. I want to be further along before we make a big announcement."

"Does Jack know?" Rod asked.

"Not yet," Alex said. "He's one of the ones that we're going to wait to tell when we're further along. But I'm betting he's going to be pretty excited. He's been asking for either a little brother or a puppy."

"Yeah, I'm betting that a puppy might have been easier, but at least this way, I won't have to walk a dog," Nova teased.

"We can still get him a puppy if you're still not sure," Alex offered.

"Right because we need a newborn and a puppy," she sassed. "I think we should figure out the newborn first and then, maybe when Jack's older and can help with a puppy, we'll revisit that plan." Hearing the two of them talk about their growing family and everyday little things like getting a puppy, made Evie long for those things in her life. As if he could read her mind, Rod reached for her hand, giving it a squeeze. She looked at their joined hands and then up to him, to find him smiling at her like a loon.

"Should we go in?" he asked. "I'm ready to kick my brother's ass at some board games."

"I'm betting that they don't play Candy Land, Rod. That's more your speed, so don't get your hopes up," Alex teased. Evie followed the three of them to Tyler's porch, never letting go of Rod's hand. She was trying to not think about all of the things that could possibly go wrong, but Evie knew that a million things could. All they had to do was get through game night and then, she'd sit down with Rod and come up with some rules for whatever this thing was that was happening between them.

RODRICK

It was nice seeing Evie so happy. She was surrounded by her friends and that was new for him. He only had a few close friends—mostly, his brother and Luke. It was fun to hang out with new people. They spent the evening eating, drinking, and just plain acting silly. He hadn't really played games since he and Alex were kids, and they were trying to kill time. Whenever he or Alex were grounded from television, they broke out the board games. It usually ended up with a fist fight and more television timeout, but they were both hardheaded jerks when they were teens.

"I'm going to grab a beer out of the kitchen," Rod said. "Can I get anyone else one?" Everyone put their hands up and he chuckled. "I'll make a few trips then," he joked.

"No need," Alex insisted. "I'll come with you and give you a hand."

Rod knew that by giving him a hand, his brother meant that he was going to be grilling him about what he had found him and Evie doing in the car. "Thanks," Rod said. He knew that sooner or later, he'd have to explain this whole mess to his brother and Nova, but he was hoping to sit down with Evie first to decide what they were doing together. He was hoping that she'd help give him some clarity about what the two of them were doing, but he was sure that she was just as clueless as he was.

Rod followed Alex into the fridge and took the three bottles of beer that he handed him. Alex shut the door and turned on his brother. "What the hell was that out in your car?" he asked.

"I think it was pretty self-explanatory. I told you that I like her, and well, I think she likes me too. Has Nova said that she suspects anything?" he asked.

"No," Alex breathed. "In fact, when we pulled up here and found the two of you, she actually squealed and clapped. She's really excited that you both are together. I am too if I'm being honest. Now, I won't have to lie to my wife and keep a secret. If you two are together, then you're technically not lying to Nova."

"That's what I told Evie, but I'm not sure if she's on board or not. We're going back to her place after this is over and talking things through," Rod said.

"Is that code for sex?" Alex asked. He wasn't about to tell his brother that Evie was a virgin, and he wouldn't pressure her for sex until she was ready. Hell, he didn't know if that was something that she'd even want with him. Maybe she had some crazy notion to save herself for marriage and that would be a shame because Rod had no intention of getting married any time soon.

"No," Rod breathed, "it's not a code for sex. Listen, I appreciate you keeping our little secret, but with any luck, it won't be something you have to keep for much longer."

"Good to know," Alex said. "But sooner or later, you and Evie will have to come clean with Nova."

"You guys coming back with those beers?" Nova asked.

"What do you care?" Rod asked. "You can't drink them anyway," he said.

"See, this is why we had to tell everyone about me being pregnant tonight. You all would have given me hell for not drinking tonight."

"You're right," Tyler agreed. "Plus, we're super excited about meeting him or her in eight months."

"We are too," Alex said. He handed out the bottles of beer and sat down next to Nova, pulling her against his side. Watching the two of them made Rod feel a bit jealous. He had to admit, he really never thought about settling down until he saw how happy it made his older brother. He still didn't have any immediate plans to get married, but he was at least thinking about it for his long-term plan.

"Have you two ever thought about having kids?" Evie asked Tyler and Doug.

"We have, but it's not as easy for us. We'll either have to find a good adoption agency or a surrogate that we can trust. Either way, we'll need a damn good lawyer to navigate our way through the mountains of paperwork that will accompany either option."

"You're in luck," Nova teased. "We happen to know a really good firm you can work with and I'm betting that you'll be able to get the friends and family discount."

"Then we're one step closer to our dream," Tyler said, smiling over at Doug. The two of them were unexpected for Rod. He wasn't sure that he'd feel comfortable around them—not because they were two guys, but because they had such a tight relationship with Evie. He worried that Tyler would spill the beans about their secret, but he hadn't yet. Plus, he seemed super protective of Evie and Rod couldn't blame the guy. He was beginning to feel the same way about her. After spending the last week with her, he'd never do anything to intentionally hurt her. Now, all the two of them had to do was find a way to navigate a path forward, and he was sure that he'd never have to face down her two angry best friends for breaking her heart because Rod never planned on doing that to Evie.

THEY STAYED past eleven and Rod was exhausted. He drove Evie home and when she turned to ask him if he still wanted to come in, he threw his plans out the window and wanted to turn her down. He was going to insist that he was tired and ask her for a raincheck. He was being a giant chicken and he knew that if he went into her house with her, he might push her for something more than talking. He didn't want to take that chance with her—the chance of hurting her because he could be a demanding asshole. But when he opened his mouth to tell her that he'd changed his mind about talking, he found himself saying that he'd love to come in for a bit.

Rod followed Evie to her front porch, trying to be patient as she fiddled with her keys, nervously trying to unlock the front door. "Here, I can get that for you," he offered. He held out his hand to her and Evie handed him the keys.

"I guess I'm a little bit nervous," she admitted.

"I'll admit, I am too," he said, unlocking the door. "But remember, we're just talking, honey," he reminded.

She stepped into the open door and took her keys back from him, letting her fingers brush his hand, and he felt those same damn sparks that he had when he kissed her earlier that night. "What if I don't want to just talk?" she whispered.

"Don't tease me, Evie," he growled. "You don't have to make me any promises you don't want to keep. I know that you're a virgin, and I won't press you for anything." He wanted to get down on his fucking knees and beg her to have sex with him, but that wasn't a part of the bargain that he had struck with her.

"How about we talk about this while we—you know, talk," she teased. "Want some coffee?" she asked. When he hired her, she said that she would never fetch his coffee for him.

"I thought that you making me coffee was off the table," he teased.

"Well, we aren't at work, so do you want some?" she asked.

"Sure," he agreed. "I'm tired, so coffee would be great."

"How about we sit in my family room?" she asked. "That way we can keep the feeling relaxed. I'm already a bundle of nerves." Rod took the two coffee mugs that she had pulled down from her and put them down on the counter. He pulled her into his arms and sealed his mouth over hers, loving the way that she sighed against his lips.

Rod ended the kiss and smiled down at her. "Still nervous?" he asked.

"No," she whispered. "How do you do that?" she asked.

"Do what?" he questioned.

"Calm me," she breathed. "You just have this crazy effect on me. You calm my nerves and make me feel like everything's going to be all right."

"It will be all right—no matter what happens, honey," he said.

"Well, you haven't run off since I told you that I'm a virgin," she said. "That's a big deal since most guys take off as soon as they hear that word."

"They were morons, Evie," Rod said. "I have to admit, the thought of you being a virgin scares the shit out of me.

I've never been with a virgin, and I'd never want to hurt you."

"You won't hurt me, Rod," she said.

"Thanks for the vote of confidence, honey," he said. "I'm just trying to figure out how someone who looks like you never lost her virginity."

"Honestly, I was focused on my schooling," she admitted. "I graduated early from high school. I was always bright and then, I started college when I was only sixteen. At first, I commuted, but then, I met Nova and Tyler and moved into their apartment. It worked out for me because they kind of looked out for me. I knew that I was a lot younger than most college girls, but once word got around, most guys treated me as though I had the plague. They avoided me at all costs. I started dating guys from town, avoiding college guys and when the notorious third date hit, they asked me to jump into bed with them, and when I admitted to being a virgin, I never heard from them again. They dropped me back at my dorm room and made me the promise of calling me in a day or so, but nothing ever happened. I guess I resigned myself to being a virgin forever, you know? I started law school and decided to become a paralegal instead of a lawyer and graduated early. I'm only twenty-two," she admitted.

"Yeah," he breathed. "I saw that on your paperwork. It's also one of the reasons why I told myself to steer clear of you. I'm twenty-nine and convinced myself that you're too young for me."

She giggled, handing him his coffee. "Come on, let's sit in the family room and you can tell me about how an old man like you became a lawyer," Evie teased. He followed her into the small room and sat on her sofa, loving the way she sat right next to him, her leg touching his as if she was comfortable with him already.

"Well, I didn't always know that I wanted to be a lawyer. My grandfather was in oil and came from old money. He left my brother and me very well off, and I didn't think about doing much of anything. I didn't have to, honestly. I traveled and had way more fun than was legally acceptable to have. My brother had become a lawyer like our old man, and together, they tried to intervene on my good time." He loved that his brother and father cared about him, but he didn't need them telling him what to do with the rest of his life.

"Well, it seems that they broke through to you," Evie said. "I mean, you're a lawyer now."

"Yeah, they wore me down. At first, I stubbornly refused to listen to a word that they were saying, but after a while, I looked into going to college and eventually law school and realized that it fit me. I decided to go, not telling either of them about my decision until I had my first two years of school under my belt."

"You kept it a secret?" she asked. "Boy, you were really stubborn."

"Still am," he said. "I guess that's why I was all right

with keeping Nova in the dark. I don't like being told what to do with my life, you know?"

"I do," she agreed. "I fought Nova for weeks when she tried to throw us together."

"Are you happy that you've changed your mind?" he asked.

"I am," she admitted. "I got a pretty good job out of the deal," she teased.

"Hey," he grumbled.

"Well, this thing between us is kind of new, so I'm not really sure what to call it or how I feel about it," Evie admitted. He felt the same way, but he was willing to see where this thing ended up if she was.

"Are you willing to give this thing a chance?" he asked.

"Yeah, but we're going to need to give it some kind of parameters," she said.

"You mean rules, right?" he asked.

"Yes, and I'd like to know exactly what I'm getting into with you, Rod. Is this going to be a real relationship or are we still faking things for Nova?"

"It's real," he breathed. "My feelings for you are real, Evie."

"What about work?" she asked. "Will we be able to keep this and work separate?"

"If that's what you'd like to do," he agreed. "I'm fine with keeping our relationship a secret."

"So, it's a relationship then?" she asked.

"I'd like to call it that, if you're good with that term," he said. Rod was beginning to feel as though he was negotiating an arbitration. Next, he'd offer to draw up a contract and he wondered if that's what it would take to get Evie to trust him.

"I am good with calling it a relationship," she agreed. "And for now, I'd like to keep it and work separate."

"Deal," he agreed. He held out his hand to her and she placed hers into his and shook. Rod pulled her against his body and kissed her, ignoring the fact that they were both holding their half-full coffee mugs still.

"Shoot," she mumbled. "I spilled coffee all over both of us."

"Not a problem," he insisted, looking down at his wet shirt. He pulled it off and tossed it to the floor, loving the way she looked his upper body over. "You might want to get out of that shirt too, honey," he said.

"I've never taken my shirt off in front of a guy before," she whispered.

"There's always a first time, honey," he said. "For everything."

"Subtle," she said.

He took her coffee mug from her and set it next to his on the table. "I won't push you, Evie. We can take this at your pace." He gently kissed her lips and she nodded and stood, tugging her shirt up over her head revealing her lacy black bra she had hidden underneath.

"You're sexy as fuck, honey," Rod breathed.

"Really?" she questioned, looking down her body. Rod reached up and pulled her down on top of his body.

"Really," he assured.

"Are we still talking?" she asked.

"That depends on you, honey," he said. "What do you want to do?"

"Um," she squeaked. "I think I'd like to make out." Rod chuckled and nodded, "Done deal, honey." He pulled her down and kissed her, sure that he'd never get enough of his secret new assistant.

EVIE

Evie wasn't sure if she was doing anything right and admitting that to Rod was going to be super embarrassing, but she wanted to get this right. If she was reading all his signs right, he was offering to be her first, and she was very willing to take him up on his offer.

"I'm not really sure what I'm doing here, Rod," she admitted.

"You're doing great, baby. Just follow your gut and if something doesn't feel right, just tell me," he offered.

"I'm afraid that I won't know if something feels right or not," she admitted. "Will you tell me what to do?"

"I think that I can do better than tell you what to do, Evie. I'll show you," he offered. She shyly nodded her head and Rod stood and lifted her into his arms.

"What are you doing?" she squealed.

"Where's your bedroom?" he asked.

"Around the corner, past the kitchen," she breathed. She wasn't sure what she had just agreed to by basically giving him permission to take her back to her bedroom, but she was sure that whatever it was, she wanted it.

"All you have to do is tell me to stop if you don't like something that I'm doing," he reminded.

"Okay," she whispered against his neck. "I can do that," she agreed. He walked with her into her bedroom and laid her across her bed. She reached for him and he shook his head at her.

"I want to look at you, Evie," he said. He looked her over and she wasn't sure what to do. She felt so self-conscious, she wanted to hide. Evie started to cross her arms over her chest and Rod growled, "Don't." She immediately pulled her arms back down to her side and watched him for whatever his next move might be.

"Have you ever had an orgasm?" he asked.

"Um, not one that I haven't given myself," she admitted. God, this was embarrassing, and Evie wondered how she'd ever look him in the eyes come Monday morning in the office.

"That's hot," he breathed. "The thought of you touching yourself makes me hard," Rod admitted. "But we'll get to that."

"I can't touch myself in front of you, Rod," she insisted.

"You can and you will, just not right now," he ordered. "Right now, I want to be the first man to give you an orgasm," he said.

"Oh," she breathed. "I'm not on the pill. Do you have a condom?" she asked.

"You won't need either," Rod insisted. "My pants are going to be staying on." She wanted to ask him if he meant permanently, but she refrained.

"You're going to touch me?" she whispered.

"Yes," he breathed, running his big hands up her jean-clad thighs. "And I'm going to taste you—here," he said, cupping her sex.

"No one's done that to me, Rod," she said. Sure, she had fantasized about a man doing that to her, but never dreamt that it would happen.

"Are you good with me doing that to you, honey?" he asked.

"I am," she said, not having to think about her answer. She wanted everything that Rod was willing to give to her.

He stood over her body, quickly unzipping her jeans and working them down her body along with her panties. He kissed his way up her body and unclasped her bra, leaving her completely bare for him. Rod took his time to look her body over and this time, she didn't want to hide from him. He looked at her as though she was a goddess. No one had ever made her feel so sexy.

"You're beautiful, Evie," he whispered. She watched as

Rod settled between her legs and he looked as though he was inspecting her, up close and personal. And when he ran his fingers through her wet folds, she nearly bucked off the bed.

Evie wasn't lying, she had touched herself, to the point of orgasm, but she'd never dreamed that just one touch from Rod could feel so good.

"You like that?" he asked.

"Yes," she hissed. She practically thrust her pussy at him, and he chuckled. "So demanding already," he teased. "I'm going to take my time and drive you crazy, honey."

"I hate to tell you this, Rod, but it won't take me very long to achieve crazy if you keep touching me like that," she whimpered.

He chuckled and touched her again, causing her to moan and ride his fingers. "Well then, this is sure to send you over the edge," he warned. She lifted her head to look down her body once more, only to watch him dip his head to lick into her pussy. God, it was the hottest thing she'd ever witnessed in her life. How could she last when he was doing what he was to her? Evie felt about ready to go off like a rocket.

"Rod," she whimpered. She couldn't stop herself from falling over the edge. It was as if she was on a speeding train and she knew that it was going to derail, but she couldn't stop it. Evie shouted out his name and he stood and smiled down at her.

"Wait here, honey," he said. He went into her master bathroom and returned with a washcloth.

"What are you doing?" she asked.

"I want to take care of you," he insisted.

She tried to wave him off, "I can take care of myself, Rod."

"Honey, if we're going to have sex someday, you're going to have to learn to let me take care of you," he insisted. He spread her folds and used the warm, wet washcloth to clean her up. It was the most intimate thing anyone had ever done to or for her, and he had just had his mouth on her pussy.

"Here," he said, "get under the covers, so you don't get cold."

"I'm not cold," she insisted. "Are you going to take off your clothes now?" she asked.

"Yes," he agreed. He ran back to the bathroom and came back out in just his boxers, his erection tenting the fabric. Rod helped her under the covers and slid in next to her. Evie wasn't sure if she was excited or scared out of her mind. Rod had promised to take care of her, and that's exactly what he had done. She was hoping that now, it would be her chance to make him feel just as good. Evie just had to figure out how to do that.

Rod pulled her against his body, his erection pressing into her ass, and kissed her shoulder. "Night, honey," he said.

"Night?" she questioned. "What the hell does that mean, Rod?" she asked.

"It's an abbreviated way to say, 'Good night,'" he said.

"I know what it's an abbreviation for, Rod," she hissed. "I'm just wondering why you're saying it to me. I thought that we were going to have sex," she said.

"Not tonight," he said around a yawn. "I'm beat."

"You can't just do what you did to me and then tell me, 'Night,'" she insisted. "Did I do something wrong?"

"No," he breathed against her neck. "You were perfect, baby," he said.

"Did you change your mind about wanting me?" she asked. "I mean, I know that I'm not perfect. Heck, the women that you usually go out with are probably beautiful and built. I'm sure that they have a lot more experience than I do, but I'm willing to learn, Rod."

He rolled her over so that she could look at him and she almost wished he hadn't. It was so much easier to have this conversation without having to look at him. "You didn't do anything wrong, honey," he said. "I promised that I wasn't going to rush you into anything that you're not ready for."

"Isn't that my decision to make?" she asked.

"It is," he said. "We'll have plenty of time to get to everything that you want to do, honey. But tonight, I just want to hold you while we sleep. We'll work our way up to sex, baby," he assured. "I promise, and when I do take you, I want for us both to be ready. I don't want to be just a guy who takes your virginity and moves on. I want to make sure that this is going to work out between the two of us. Can you hold out just a bit longer, honey?" he asked. She wanted to pout and tell him, no, but she knew that would only make her sound like a child.

"Fine," she agreed. "But I won't wait forever," she insisted.

"Noted," Rod said. "Can I hold you while we sleep?" he asked.

"Will you spend the whole night?" she asked.

"If you'll allow me to, yes," he said.

"I'd like that, Rod." She felt so raw and emotionally charged. Having him there felt right. She wasn't lying earlier when she told him that he had some strange calming effect on her. She loved that about him and telling him to hit the road now didn't feel right to her. Evie flipped back over and snuggled into his arms, wiggling her ass against his impressive erection.

"You keep doing that, I won't make good on my promise to hold off on making you mine." She liked the thought of him making her his. Just hearing him say the word, "Mine" come out of his mouth, made her hot.

"I like it when you say that," she whispered.

"Say what?" he asked.

"When you call me yours," Evie said.

"Would you like to be mine, honey?" he asked.

"I think that I would," she admitted.

"Good to know, honey," Rod said. "Night."

"Good night, Rod," she whispered back over her shoulder. As soon as Evie closed her eyes, she could feel herself slipping into sleep. She usually had trouble falling to sleep, but tonight, she couldn't seem to stay awake, and she was sure that it had everything to do with the sexy man behind her.

RODRICK

Rod woke up wrapped in soft, warm woman. He had never spent the night at a woman's place before. Hell, if he went home with a woman, he'd fuck her and run the hell out of there, going home to sleep in his own bed. He believed that if he slept with a woman overnight, he'd get attached, and he was right. He was already starting to become attached to Evie after spending a little more than a week with her. She had him rethinking his whole stance on not getting involved with anyone.

Evie was practically on top of him, her arms draped across his chest and her legs spread eagle over his legs. His cock was all for waking up plastered against a hot woman, even if he wasn't going to get his way and be able to take Evie today. He was being honest when he told her that he wanted to take things slowly with her. There was no way that he'd have sex with her until she was ready, and she wouldn't be ready to be with him until he could prove to Evie that he was worthy. Even if he wasn't, he just needed her to believe that he was.

"Hey," she breathed, looking up at him. Evie quickly rolled off of him and pulled the sheets over her body. "Sorry," she said. "I didn't mean to lay on top of you. I guess I have boundary issues when I sleep."

"I didn't mind," he said. "In fact, I kind of like waking up with you wrapped around me."

"Oh," she whispered. "Well, thanks for staying the night," she said. He hated how nervous she sounded. That was the last thing he wanted her to feel. Hot, turned on, and wanted—sure. Nervous, no.

"It's just me, honey," Rod whispered, pulling her in for a quick kiss.

"I know," she breathed, "it's just the first time that I've woken up with a man in my bed. This is just all so new for me, you know?"

"If we're being completely honest, honey, this is a first for me too. I don't spend the night at a woman's place and I certainly don't invite them over to spend the night with me," Rod admitted.

"You've never spent the night with a woman?" she asked. "But you've had sex, right?"

He smirked over at her and she giggled. "Yes, I've had sex," he grumbled. "But when we're done, I usually take off and go back to my house. I never wanted to give the woman the wrong idea."

"Gee," she breathed. "That's so sweet," she teased.

"Well, I thought it was," he griped. "What's wrong with not wanting to lead a woman on?"

"Nothing, but why sleep with her then?" she asked. "I mean, I understand the why of it, but why treat me any differently?" That was a question that he wasn't sure that he was ready to answer yet.

"I'm not sure, really," he admitted. "It just feels different with you. Maybe it's because your Nova's friend and she'll kill me if I fuck this up with you, but I want to do things the right way with you, honey," he admitted.

"That's sweet," she said. "Even the part about Nova killing you," she teased.

"Thanks," he grumbled. "But it's the truth."

"Speaking of truths," she said. "We never really discussed what we're going to do about telling Nova the truth about us." She was right, they hadn't discussed that yet, but he was hoping that avoiding the topic might be the way to go.

"I say that we see what happens with us before we spill our guts to Nova. I mean, right now, we're technically not lying to her, right?" he asked.

Evie sighed and nodded, "Right," she agreed. "But we started off lying to her and that still doesn't feel right. I just want to come clean with her and let the chips fall where they might."

"Listen, I won't tell you that you can't tell your friend the truth. I'd just like a little bit of time for us," he said. "Just the two of us to try to figure this thing out."

"All right," she agreed. "I'll give us two weeks to get our shit together and then, I'm telling Nova everything."

He nodded, "That sounds very fair, honey, thank you."

"I'm not doing this for you, Rod. I'm doing it for us. I'd like to see where this thing ends up too," she admitted.

"So, what would you like to do today?" he asked.

"Today?" she asked. "Don't you have things you want to do at your place?" she asked.

"Well, unless you want to spend the day naked, in bed, I'll need to run by my place for a change of clothes," he said.

"I vote for spending the day naked, in bed," she eagerly agreed, making him laugh.

"We're going to take this slow, remember?" he asked.

She pouted at him, and he laughed again. "While I find your little pout completely adorable, I haven't changed my mind about waiting to make you mine." She shivered and he pulled her against his body. "You cold?" he asked.

"No," she said. "It's just hearing you call me yours again, does crazy things to me," she admitted.

"Well, staying in bed with you naked isn't going to be a good idea," he said. "Not if you keep saying sexy things like that to me."

"So, what will we do then?" she asked.

"Bowling?" he asked.

"I suck at it," she admitted. Great, now all he could think about was the way she said the word suck and how much he wanted to teach her how to give a blow job. He went to sleep last night rock hard and woke up the same. He needed to get off, but he was going to wait until he was in the shower to do that.

"You all right?" she asked.

"Yeah," he lied. "I just need to get my mind out of the gutter."

"I kind of like your mind just where it is," she sassed. "You didn't—you know, last night. It wasn't fair to you."

"It was very fair to me. I enjoyed every second of eating your sweet pussy," he growled. "Watching you come was hot as fuck. I can't wait to do it again."

"Me too," she admitted. "But I think that you need something first." Evie ran her hands over his erection, and he moaned. If she kept touching him that way, he wouldn't be able to tell her to stop.

"Is that okay?" she asked.

"It's more than okay," he admitted. She brazenly pulled down his boxers and dipped her hands inside to find his cock. Her hands felt like velvet running over his shaft. Rod shamelessly moaned and thrust himself into her hands, needing more.

"That feels so fucking good," he said.

"I'd like to taste you," she said. "The way that you did me. Will you teach me?" she asked.

"Yes," he hoarsely breathed. Evie eagerly sat up and shimmied over to his lap, practically straddling him.

"You seem eager," he teased.

"Well, I'm an eager student. Teach me what to do," she demanded, pulling his boxers the rest of the way down his legs, tossing them to the floor.

"Grab my cock down by the root," he demanded. "Pump me with both hands and then, suck me into your mouth. Take as much as you can of me. You'll have to find a rhythm of hands and mouth, but once you do, you'll be great."

"Fingers crossed," she said. She did exactly what he told her to do and God, her mouth felt fantastic. She sucked him to the back of her throat and then worked her way back up his shaft. He knew that he wouldn't last very long if she kept doing things like that to him. He was already on edge from last night still. He was about ready to explode, and he worried that he'd do it down her pretty little throat.

"I hate to say this, honey, but you need to stop," he said. "I'm going to come." She seemed to dig in her heels, pumping him harder and sucking him deeper, like a woman on a mission. "Evie," he shouted in warning, but it was too late. He was already coming into her mouth, and she swallowed everything he gave her, wiping her lips after she licked him clean, and he was sure that it was the hottest thing he had ever seen.

"Was that okay?" she asked.

"Jesus, honey," he breathed. He sounded as though he had just run a marathon and damn if he didn't feel that way too. "If it was any better, I'd be dehydrated right now." She giggled and laid back down next to him, cuddling into his side.

"You're a quick study," he teased.

"I told you that I was," she said. "I excel at academics," she teased. "I think that I might be ready for my next lesson."

"Well, I'm not sure what else I can teach you, honey," he said. "Besides us having sex, I think you've pretty much mastered the rest of it."

"Oh," she said. "Well then, let's have sex," she said.

"I have an idea," he said. "How about a shower—together, and then you let me make you some breakfast."

"I don't have much here," she said. "Just some eggs and pancake mix."

"Well, it just so happens that I'm a wizard when it comes to making pancakes," he said. "We can spend the morning getting to know each other better."

"You've seen me naked and vice versa," she said. "I think that we know each other pretty well, don't you?"

"That's just physical stuff," he countered. "I'm talking about the actual getting to know each other part of things. I want to know more about you, Evie," he said.

"I'd like to know more about you too, Rod," she admitted. That was good because he knew that just sex never lasted, and he wanted something that lasted with Evie.

"HOW ABOUT A SHOWER FIRST?" he asked, getting out of bed. He loved the way that she looked him over.

"You work out, don't you?" she asked.

"Just about every day." It was one of the reasons why he had built a home gym, in his penthouse. He liked being able to work out whenever he wanted, and he hated the crowds at regular gyms. So, he took his brother's idea and built his own state-of-the-art gym. "I have a home gym, so I can work out whenever I want."

"Wow," she breathed. "That would be awesome. I used to work out at that gym downtown, but after losing my job, I had to drop my membership."

"I'm sorry," he said. "I hate that you lost your job because you helped Alex and Nova. You did the right thing though," he assured.

"Thanks for saying that," she said. "I couldn't sit back and let Nova's scumbag ex take Jack from her. I needed to help her get him back, even at the cost of my job. I know that she'd do the same for me."

"I'm sure she would," he agreed. That was just who his sister-in-law was. She was the sweetest person he'd ever met.

"Come on," he said, holding out his hand for her. "Let's take our shower so that I can make us some breakfast—I'm starving."

"I am too," she admitted. She took his hand and let him

pull from the bed. As soon as her feet hit the floor, he scooped her up and carried her to the bathroom.

"Honestly, Rod," she griped, "I can walk."

"I know, but this is so much more fun, honey," he said. "I like having your naked body against mine." He let her slide down his body to stand in front of the shower. He turned it on and waited for it to get hot, while Evie grabbed some towels. He couldn't believe that he was about to ask her this, but it was all he could think about since he woke up—well, and had a mind-blowing orgasm.

"Spend the night with me at my place tonight," he said.

"Your place?" she asked.

"Yeah, I have to go home to grab a change of clothes and clothes for tomorrow. Instead of going back and forth, pack a bag and spend the night at my place tonight." She looked him over and he was sure that she was going to tell him no.

"I thought that you said that you don't have women spend the night at your place," she reminded.

"I don't," he said. "But I want to have you spend the night at my place, Evie."

She smiled at him and nodded, and Rod let out the breath that he didn't know he was holding. "I'd love to spend the night at your place, Rod," she agreed.

"Thank you, honey," he said.

"You still have to make me breakfast," she teased, stepping into the hot spray of water.

"Already setting conditions to our relationship," he

teased. He swatted her ass, "Move over, honey," he ordered. He climbed into the shower and wrapped his arms around her, trying to steal all the hot water, making her giggle. He liked seeing her so happy. He helped to soap up her body, loving all of her breathy little sighs and moans, and then he moved on to washing her hair for her. He liked her new shorter style that she had gone with after Nova's wedding.

"What made you cut off your hair?" he asked.

She shrugged, "I kept it long for Nova's wedding, and then I was just over it. I needed a change. So many things were uncertain in my life, I just needed something that I could control, you know?" she asked. He did understand that. It was how he felt about his life since passing the bar. He felt as though he had been spiraling out of control and honestly, Evie was one of the first things that had him feeling grounded in a damn long time.

"I like it this way," he admitted. "I mean, you look hot either way, but I like it shorter."

"Thanks," she said. "I wasn't sure about it until I realized how much easier it was to do when it's short." He gently held her back into the spray of the shower and let the water rinse the shampoo from her hair. Rod quickly soaped up his body, shampooed his hair, and rinsed off. He turned off the water and grabbed a towel to wrap her in, and did the same for himself, wrapping it around his waist.

"How about if you take your time up here and get dressed and I'll make us some breakfast?" he asked.

"I don't need much time to get ready," she assured. "Besides, I'd kind of like to help with breakfast."

"Are you one of those people who get bent out of shape if their kitchen gets messed up?" he teased. She looked at him defiantly and he knew he had guessed correctly. Rod couldn't help but chuckle as he pulled her in for a quick kiss. "Okay, honey," he agreed. "You can help me make breakfast. Come on, let's get dressed."

EVIE

Evie wasn't sure why Rod was taking his good, sweet time to have sex with her. Sure, the orgasms were nice, and the foreplay was great, but she was ready for the real thing.

She pulled on her clothes, quickly dried her hair, applied what she liked to call her weekend makeup, and met Rod in the kitchen. He was sitting at her table, having a cup of coffee, waiting for her.

"You didn't start without me," she said.

"Nope." He got up and poured her a cup of coffee, handing it to her. "I'm sorry, but I don't know how you like it."

"I have special creamers in the fridge. I like just a splash of cream with my very strong coffee," she said. "And you don't need to be sorry about not knowing how I take my coffee," she insisted. "We're only just getting to know each other's likes, dislikes, and little quirks."

"For example, you don't like anyone in your kitchen, because they might mess it up," Rod said.

"Right," she agreed. "And you like to drive me crazy by not having sex with me," she said.

"It's not like that, Evie," he said. "You know that I want to take my time with you and get to know you. I don't want to fuck this up."

"I get that, but I want this, Rod. You can't fuck it up," she assured. "How about tonight, at your place?" she asked.

"That's a bit soon, don't you think? We're still getting to know each other," he said.

"Well, I figured that we could speed up the process," she offered. "Kind of like speed dating."

"Oh, this is going to be interesting," Rod drawled.

"I know that your accent is Scottish, when did you come to live in America?" she asked.

"When I was just a kid, about seven if memory serves. My brother was a lot older and that's why his accent is much more defined than mine," he said. She thought that both of their accents were hot, but Rod's was softer, almost hidden even. When he barked orders at her on how to give him a blowjob, she could hear his Scottish lilt and she had to admit, it made her wet. And the way that he said her name, made her want to rip off her clothes and demand that he have sex with her right here and now.

"You have that look again," he said.

"What look is that?" she asked.

"The one that tells me that you're thinking about the two of us getting naked again," he said. He wasn't wrong, but there was no way that she'd admit that to him.

"Um, why did your parents come to America and bring you and Alex?" she asked, trying to change the topic.

"Subtle," he chided. "They came here at my grandfather's request. He was my dad's father and one day, out of the blue, he called my dad and told him that he was dying and that we needed to come to America right away."

"Oh no," Evie said, "that's awful."

"Yeah, you would think so, but the old bugger lied and ended up living for another ten years. My family ended up staying and my father opened his own firm here in town. Mom was a teacher, so she got her certificate to teach here, and she loved America, so that made things easier on my dad. The great part was that Alex and I got to know our grandfather—something that we wouldn't have had if we had stayed in Scotland."

"He's the one who left you two all your money, right?" she asked.

"Yep," he said. "I really liked the guy."

"Was he Scottish too?" she asked.

"No," Rod said. "My grandfather was American. He lived in Scotland for a bit after he graduated from college. He didn't do much, in the way of work. He liked to travel. I guess I'm like him in that regard. Anyway, he met my grandmother while he was living in Scotland, and they got married and had my dad. She died when my father graduated from high school and started college and my grandpa just couldn't stay in Scotland. He told my dad that there were too many memories there haunting him, and he moved back to America. My dad went back and forth between college in Scotland, and America, but he met my mom during his last semester at school and ended up staying in Scotland."

"Your family sounds very interesting," she said.

"How about yours?" he asked.

"Well, my mom and stepdad live out west, in Montana, still. It's originally where I'm from. My mom is the person who pushed me to graduate early and go to college. She was great. She didn't fight to keep me at home when she knew that I needed a little extra push. I never really knew my father. He took off on my mom and me after I was born and she met my stepdad, Stephen. I've always considered him my dad since I don't remember my own."

"I'm glad that you had your stepdad," he said. Evie watched as he finished up making the pancake mix and took the bowl from him.

"Thanks," she said. "If you work on the eggs, I'll finish the pancakes." She had the griddle hot and ready for the first batch.

"Deal," he said, grabbing the eggs from the fridge. "Did you know your grandparents?" he asked.

"Nope," she said. "My mom's parents both died before

I was born, and we really don't know much about my father's parents."

"That's kind of sad," Rod said.

"Yeah, but it's hard to miss something that you never had," she insisted.

He shrugged, "I guess."

She flipped the pancakes and put them onto a plate once they were finished. "How are the eggs coming?" she asked.

"Just about finished," he said. He was scrambling them over the stove, and she had to admit, a man who could cook was sexy as hell.

"After we eat, would you mind packing so that we can head over to my place? I'd love a change of clothes," he said.

"Sure," she agreed. She was actually looking forward to seeing where Rod lived. She knew that he lived in town, in one of the high rises, but that was about it. "I can't wait to see your place," she admitted.

"It's not like Alex's house," he said. "I like things a little bit lower key," he said.

"Well, I think that low key suits you, Rod," she said. "Pancakes are ready," she said, proudly holding up the platter.

"So are the eggs. Let's eat. The sooner we finish breakfast, the sooner I can show you my place, and then, we can get to the part you've been waiting for," he promised.

"The sex?" she asked.

"Yep—the sex, honey," he agreed. Honestly, Evie couldn't wait.

THEY SPENT the morning eating and talking over breakfast, getting to each other better—although she liked thinking of it more like speed dating. He helped her clean the dishes and pack, and she had to admit, she was surprised that he was so hands-on. She knew that Rod could have people do all of those things for him, but he pitched in and gave her a hand.

After she was all packed and ready to leave, he loaded her overnight back into his SUV, insisting that she leave her car behind to ride with him. She was going to balk at his idea, but she liked the thought of spending extra time with him. He promised to run her home whenever she wanted and to even take her to work in the morning. Evie wasn't sure if she liked the idea of everyone seeing them arriving to work together, but he promised it wouldn't be a big deal.

Once they got to his penthouse, he carried her bags up to his bedroom and dumped them on the sofa. "I'd like for you to stay in my bed—with me," he said. "But I don't want to assume that you'll be all right with that."

She went up on her tiptoes and kissed him. "Thank you for not assuming, but I'd love to sleep in your bed with you, Rodrick." She wanted to remind him that he had promised that they could have sex once they were at his place, but she didn't want to seem too pushy. She had already done enough pushing. Hell, she had been begging, but she wanted to try to let things just happen if that was what Rod wanted.

"Good," he said, pulling her down onto the bed with him. "Because I say we get into my bed right now."

"Oh," she breathed. "I'd like that," she agreed.

"Naked," he added.

"Naked?" she squeaked. He had already seen her body, but still, it was new for her. She suddenly felt hot all over, and she knew that if she stayed in her clothing, she'd burn up alive with the way that he was touching her.

"I want you naked, honey," he said.

"Will you be naked too?" she asked.

"Yes," he whispered into her ear. "I want you, Evie."

"I want you too, Rod," she admitted. "I take it we're skipping the tour you promised me," she teased. He rolled away from her, and she grabbed onto his waist. "Where are you going?"

"Well, if you would rather have the tour now, we can do that instead," he agreed.

"No," she shouted. "I can wait for the tour."

Rod chuckled and rolled back on top of her, "Then, let's get you naked." He made quick work of stripping her bare and by the time they were both completely naked, she was wet and ready for whatever he had planned next. Evie just hoped that this time, he wouldn't stop before making her his completely, because it was all she could think about.

RODRICK

Rod tried to maintain his cool, but all he wanted to do was thrust balls deep inside of Evie. He needed to remember that she was a virgin and to take his time with her, no matter how much she was begging him to make her his.

"I want to make this good for you, honey," Rod whispered.

"I just want you, Rod," she breathed. "It's going to hurt, either way, right?" she asked. He had no clue, but he had heard that it might.

"I don't know, honey," he admitted.

"Please, just make me yours," she begged. He ran his fingers through her slick folds, feeling how wet she was turned him on completely.

"See," she said. "I'm ready," she promised. She felt more than ready, but he wouldn't just force his way into her like an animal. He slid first one and then another finger into her core, stretching her, getting her ready to take his cock. She moaned and moved against his hand, taking everything that he was giving her. "I need more," she begged as he stroked his thumb over her clit. She cried out again and this time, new wetness coated his hand as she came for him. She was so new to all of this, but even just a few touches from him set her off. Rod thought that Evie was the hottest woman he'd ever been with as she shamelessly road his hand taking her pleasure from him.

He knew that she was as ready as she was going to be for him, but he hated having to do this next part. "Do you want me to go slow and easy or fast, to get it over with?" he asked.

She looked up at him through her sex-fueled haze and smiled. "Fast," she breathed. "Just do it, Rod." She wrapped her arms around his shoulders and pulled him down for a kiss as he lined up his cock to her drenched opening.

"I'm sorry if this hurts, baby," he whispered against her lips. He thrust into her body and filled her as she cried out. It took everything in him to be still, giving her time to adjust to him being inside of her.

"You feel so big inside of me," she whimpered.

"Are you all right?" he asked.

"I will be, just give me another minute," she promised. He kissed her as she panted through the pain, working his way down her neck and when he dipped his head to suck one of her taut nipples into his mouth, she moaned and wiggled underneath of him.

"I'm good," she insisted.

"Thank God, because I need to move," he said. He pulled almost all the way out of her and thrust back into her body, causing her to moan again. He took that as a good sign that she was all right and kept going.

"It feels so good," she whispered. "I'm so close." Rod was close too, but he knew that he couldn't find his release without her getting off first. He snaked his hand down between where their bodies were joined and let his thumb strum over her clit. It didn't take Evie long before she was going off like a firecracker, shouting out his name again. He loved how natural she looked when she found her release. Evie wasn't worried about it being her first time or doing something wrong, she was in the moment with him, soaking up all of the pleasure that he was giving her.

"Baby," he crooned. He kissed her like he was going to consume her and when she panted into his mouth, unable to control the second orgasm that ripped through her body, he found his own release, riding it out until he knew that she had finished. When they were both done, he collapsed onto the mattress next to her and pulled her into his side. Evie felt so right there, he was sure that he would never find anyone else to fill that space. She belonged next to him —forever if she'd have him. But telling her that now, after he took her virginity would only sound like a cheesy line, and he wouldn't do that to her.

"I'm yours now, Rod," she said around a yawn.

"You're mine now, baby," he agreed. She just had no idea how much he meant what he had just said, but she would soon enough.

MONDAY MORNING, he drove them both to work, loving that Evie didn't seem to mind him escorting her into the office. He thought for sure she'd bulk at the idea of him walking in with her since they had both agreed to keep work and their private lives separate. As soon as they walked through the building's front doors, she dropped his hand and while a part of him wanted to protest, Rod didn't, trying to respect the agreement that he had made with her.

"How about lunch, honey?" he asked.

"Would you mind if we ordered in? I can have it delivered and we can eat in your office. I've got a mountain of paperwork to catch up on this week," she said.

"Sounds good to me," he agreed. He didn't care where they ate, as long as he could spend some alone time with her. She nodded and stepped onto the elevator that would take her up to the top floor which housed Alex, Edon, Evie, and his offices. He loved that they had a somewhat private workspace up there and he knew that sooner or later, Evie would feel more comfortable about coming to work with him.

"Hey man," Luke said, stopping him from getting onto

the next elevator. "How have you been?" Luke was one of his closest friends and Rod felt like kind of an asshole for not making more of an effort to stay in touch with him. Since meeting Evie, all he wanted to do was spend every waking minute with her.

"Good, Luke," he said. "How are you?"

"I feel like we haven't talked in forever," Luke said.

"I know," Rod agreed. "It's my fault. I've met someone and I guess our relationship has taken me a bit by surprise."

"It's Evie, isn't it?" Luke asked.

"Shit," Rod grumbled. "I'm not supposed to tell anyone at work about us."

"I saw the two of you come in just now, holding hands in the parking lot. If you don't want anyone to know, maybe you should come to work in separate vehicles and not hold hands on your way in," Luke said.

"Where would the fun be in that?" Rod asked. "Don't tell Evie that you noticed the two of us together. She is insisting to keep work and personal stuff separate. I'd tell the whole fucking world if she'd let me."

"She's a pretty fantastic person, from what I've gotten to know about her. I talked to her the other day in the breakroom when I came up to talk to Alex." Luke was the head of their security and had meetings with Alex once a week, or more, depending on what was going on in the building. Rod liked that his best friend could work for the same company that he did. They used to have lunch together once a week, but he had really slacked off.

"We should have lunch this week and catch up," Rod offered.

"Deal," Luke said. "Um, you mind if I ask you a quick question?" he asked.

"Not at all," Rod agreed. "Shoot."

"That new girl that works for your brother, is she single?" Luke asked.

"You mean Ruby?" Alex had hired a new assistant once Nova passed the bar and became one of the firm's new junior lawyers. She was a great assistant and really kept his brother organized, but she was kind of nerdy and introverted.

"Yeah," Luke breathed. "Is she married or anything like that?"

"I don't think so, why?" Rod asked.

"Well, I didn't want to get shot down if she's married. I like to do a little bit of research on a woman before I flat out ask her out," Luke admitted.

"You're going to ask Ruby out?" Rod questioned.

"At some point," Luke said, "when I get my nerve up." Luke was a good-looking guy. He had women around that place falling all over themselves to get him just to notice them. Rod was baffled by his wanting Ruby but to each their own.

"Well, good luck, not that you'll need it. You can get a date with any woman in this place, man," Rod reminded.

"I know, but I want Ruby," Luke said. "Call me with what days you have free for lunch, and we'll make it happen," Luke said. "I've got to get back to work." He patted Rod's shoulder and disappeared back into his office.

He stepped off the elevator and found Evie in Nova's office, sitting on the sofa in there, gabbing about something. She shot him a look and he wondered if everything was all right, but he couldn't worry about them talking every time he saw them together. He tried to relax as he walked back to his office, telling himself that everything was fine. He had a crazy day ahead of him, and all Rod wanted to worry about now was getting Evie to agree to spend the night with him again tonight—and every night after, but that was something they could discuss over their lunch date.

EVIE

Evie stepped off the elevator and ran right into Nova who seemed to be waiting for her arrival. "Just the woman I've been looking for," she said. Evie wanted to run into her office, shut the door, and lock it, but she knew that sooner or later, she'd have to face her best friend.

"What's up?" Evie asked. "I have a ton of work to do." She added the last part knowing that Nova wouldn't really care about her workload, but she had to try something.

"You remember game night, when you and Rod left a little bit early, and I stayed at Tyler's place with Alex?"

"Um, sure," Evie said. Red flags were flying all around her, but there was nothing that she could do to get out of what was about to happen.

"Come with me," Nova insisted. "We need to talk and I'm betting that you'll want to do this in my office where we have some privacy." Shit—this wasn't how Evie wanted to begin her week. One of the guys had spilled the beans and now, all she was going to be able to do was come clean with her best friend.

She let Nova pull her along to her office and shut the door, pointing to her sofa. "Sit," she ordered. Evie did as Nova ordered, not willing to face any more of her wrath.

"What's this all about?" Evie asked, pretending to be in the dark. She knew exactly what this showdown was over but admitting it before Nova spilled her guts wasn't about to happen.

"You know what this is about, Evie," Nova said. "You lied to me. You let Rod lie for the both of you—you two aren't really in a relationship," she said.

"Well, that's only partially true," Evie said. "We are in a relationship, even if we weren't when Rod told you that we were. It started as a lie, but it ended up being the truth," she said. "I'm so sorry, Nova."

"Sorry?" Nova breathed. "I consider you to be like a sister and you're sorry for lying to me. You shouldn't have done it in the first place."

"You're right," Evie agreed. "I shouldn't have, but Rod asked me to give him some time and well, I like him—I really like him."

"Why did he ask you to lie for him?" Nova questioned.

"Because he didn't want you to hound him about dating me—neither of us did." Evie watched as Rod stepped free from the elevator and looked her over through the glass wall that lined Nova's office. She tried to paste on her best, "I'm all right" face, but she worried that she was failing miserably at it. He seemed to buy it enough to keep on going into his office and she breathed a sigh of relief. The last thing she needed was him getting in on this conversation. Nova would have plenty to say to him separately, but Evie just wanted to get her part over with.

"I can't believe you let him tell me that you two were together when you weren't. I can't believe you took his side," Nova scolded.

"I told you, I like him. I guess I just lost my mind a little," Evie said.

"How does he feel about you?" Nova asked.

"Um, I think he feels the same way about me," Evie said. "We've only been together, officially, for a few days. We really haven't discussed feelings yet."

"Have you thought about the fact that he could be using you? What if he's with you to keep me off of his back still?" Nova asked.

"That's not fair," Evie insisted. "He wouldn't do that to me. He knows about my track history with men. I told him that I was a virgin, and he didn't run away," Evie whispered.

"Let me guess, he's taken care of that for you, right?" Nova said. Evie didn't like the way Nova was accusing Rod of wrongdoing.

"That's none of your business, Nova," Evie spat.

"What's happening between Rod and me is my business," Evie said.

"I'm just saying if he was willing to lie to me, and I'm technically his family, then he'll lie to you too. I just want you to be careful, Evie," Nova insisted.

"I can take care of myself," Evie breathed. "Listen, I'm sorry that I lied to you. I'll apologize for my part, but I won't sit here and let you tell me that I'm not important to Rod. He's given me no reason to not trust him."

"Sure, because asking you to lie to your best friend seems trustworthy," Nova countered.

"I know that you're hurt right now, so I'm going to give you a pass, but this conversation is over," Evie said. She stood and walked out of Nova's office, keeping her tears at bay. The thought of going to her office, where Rod or Nova could follow her, wasn't a pleasant one. Instead, she headed to the elevators and took them down to the lobby. She needed some air, some time to think, and she couldn't do that up in her office.

As soon as she got outside, she called for an Uber and was picked up minutes later, before anyone even knew she was missing. They pulled out onto the highway and her cell phone rang. It was Rod and she debated if she wanted to answer it or not.

"What?" she answered her cell.

"What the hell is going on, Evie?" Rod asked. "Why did you leave?"

"Nova knows," she said. "Either Alex or Tyler told her

after we left, but she knows that we lied to her. She said that you're only with me because you're still trying to keep her off of your back. She said that you're using me."

"Baby—that's just not true," Rod insisted. "Let me come get you and we can talk this out."

"No," she spat. "I just need some time. I'll be out of the office for the rest of the day. I need to think about this and get my mind straight, please give me the time to do that, Rod."

"You can't be serious," he said. "I'd never use you, honey," he assured.

"I can't talk about this right now; I'll call you later when I have my head on straight." She ended the call and tossed her cell back into her purse, letting the sob that had bubbled up from her chest out. Had she just made the biggest mistake of her life by walking away from Rod? She knew that she might be foolish for believing Nova, but a part of her was thinking that her best friend might be onto something. Rod and she shouldn't have been together, but they were, and it felt right to her. Had he coaxed her into his bed just to make his lies the truth? Was he covering his ass with his family and using her to do it?

"Where to, Miss?" the driver asked. That was a good question. She couldn't go home. She told him to go to the only hotel she knew of in town, and he said that he knew the place. She'd spend a few nights there cleaning her head, and then, she'd figure out what to do next.

Evie pulled her cell back out of her purse and called

Nova, her call going right to voicemail. "I know I don't have the right to ask you for a favor, but I can't go home. I need some time to think about what you said. I need to know that you're not right about Rod and that he's not using me. Can you stop by my place and pack some things for me? I'm staying at the hotel down on Main Street. Please, don't tell Rod where I am, he's already called me, and I told him that I just need some time. I'm sorry, Nova," she whispered into the phone and ended the call. She was sorry too. Never in a million years did she ever see herself lying to her best friend, and now she was going to pay a heavy price.

RODRICK

Rod was determined to find Evie. It had been almost a week since she took off from the office. He hated that she told him that she just needed space. He didn't want to give her space, he wanted to know what the hell was going on—why she suddenly believed what Nova had said about him using her. How could she believe that about him?

He had looked everywhere for her. Every day, he waited for her to come into the office, and she never showed up. She had called HR and told them that she was taking some personal time but didn't give them a date that she'd be back. He was going nuts and he had a feeling that the only two people who knew where Evie was were his brother and Nova. He was done trying to figure this all out and marched into Alex's office.

"Just tell me where she is, Alex," he begged. Since she came clean and told Nova about their little ruse of faking a relationship and lying to her, she had disappeared. He knew that it had everything to do with Nova and their conversation, but neither she nor Alex were telling him where he could find Evie. He was done letting them lie to him. Rod had suffered enough, and he was going to demand answers.

"I promised my wife that I wouldn't tell you where Evie is," he said.

"I'll beg if I have to, Alex," he said. "I'm in love with her and I can't just let her go like this."

"You're in love with Evie?" Nova said, walking into Alex's office. "You forced her to lie to me, Rod. Does that sound like something you'd do to someone you love?"

"I made a wrong judgment call and drug Evie into my lie. If you want to be mad at someone, here I am, but you keeping her from me isn't the right thing to do. What would have happened if someone tried to keep you from Alex?" he asked. "Or you from Nova?" he said to his brother.

"No one could have kept me from her," Alex growled.

"I feel the same way about Evie, man," Rod admitted. "I'm in love with her. I want her to move in with me, but Nova convinced her that I'm not serious about her. What did you say to her to make her run away from me?" he asked Nova.

"I told her the truth—that a man who asks you to lie for him is bad news. My ex-husband made me lie for him all the time and look where he is now." Her ex was in prison for paying off judges and lawyers to win cases. Rod knew that he was nothing like her fucking ex-husband.

"That's not fair, Nova," Alex chided. "My brother might have told a lie to keep you from pushing him into going on more blind dates, but he's nothing like Simon. At least admit that much to be true."

"Fine," she mumbled. "I'm sorry, Rod. I guess that I just got carried away. You aren't like my ex, but you did get my very best friend to lie to me. Evie was the one person that I knew I could count on to tell me the truth. Now, I don't even have that."

"I can't apologize enough, Nova," Rod said.

"No, you can't," Nova barked.

He sighed, "But I can make you the promise that I will never ask her to lie to you again."

"Ever?" Nova asked.

"Ever," Rod agreed. "Please, just tell me where I can find her. I need to be with her."

She looked over at Alex and Rod felt as though he was holding his breath, waiting for her to make up her mind about what to do. "Fine," she grumbled. "I'll give you the address where you can find her, but if you hurt her, I'll be the one you'll have to deal with," Nova said.

"Duly noted," Rod agreed.

"She's at the hotel in town—the one on the corner of Main and Holiday Streets," she said.

"I know the one," he said. "Why did she go there?" he asked. "No, don't answer that. I'm betting she went there to try to avoid me, right?" Nova nodded and Rod pulled her in for a quick hug. "Thanks," he said.

"Don't disappoint me, Rod," Nova ordered.

"Never," he assured. He ran out of the office and onto the elevator, not wanting to waste a second getting to Evie. He was going to go get his girl and nothing would stand in his way again.

ROD PULLED into the parking lot to the hotel address that Nova gave him. He just needed to figure out which room she was in, and then, he'd find her and convince her to move in with him. Hell, he wanted to marry her, but they'd get to that.

He ran into the lobby and found what he was hoping was a friendly woman who'd find him just charming enough to give him Evie's room number.

"Hi," he said. "I'm trying to locate my girlfriend, but I can't remember what room she said she was in."

"I'm sorry sir, but it's our policy not to give out that kind of information," the woman said.

"I understand," he said. "But I need to deliver some bad news, and well, time is of the essence." The woman looked him over as if she didn't believe a word that he was saying and why should she—he was totally lying.

"Fine," he said, "if you would be so kind to deliver the message that her grandmother has passed, I'd be grateful." He looked the woman over waiting for some response from her, but she gave none. "Thanks for your time," he said, turning to leave. He made it all the way to the lobby door before she called Rod back over to the desk.

"Miss Jones is in room 328. Take the elevator around the corner to the third floor and make a left when you get off," the woman said.

"Thank you," he said. "I'm sure that Miss Jones will appreciate this." He knew for a fact that him showing up at her door was going to piss her off. He walked around the corner and got onto the elevator, following the woman at the front desk's directions.

Rod found room 328 and knocked on the door. He heard someone rummaging around the room and he swore he could hear Evie's soft curses, making him smile. She pulled open the door, "Can't you see the 'Do not disturb' sign on the door handle?" She looked him over and immediately tried to shut the door on him. Rod shoved his foot in the way and winced when the door hit it with force.

"Evie," he breathed. "Just give me a chance here," he begged.

"I can't," she said. "I still don't know how I feel about everything that's happened between us. Talking to Nova put our 'relationship' in perspective for me," she said, using air quotes around the word relationship.

"I don't know exactly what Nova said to you, but I can guess. But you should know that she's the one who told me where I could find you. She was angry that we lied to her and she put doubts in your mind about us—I get it, but you didn't have those doubts prior, right?" he asked.

She shrugged, "Not completely. I mean, I wondered if you were just with me to keep Nova off of your back, but then, when we were together, you made me forget my doubts."

"I never want you to have any doubts when it comes to me or us, honey," he said.

"I wasn't with you to keep Nova off of my back. I was with you because I like to spend time with you. Well, that and you're hot." She giggled and the sound gave him some hope that he might be getting through to her.

"I like spending time with you too," she admitted.

"That's a start," he said. Rod took a chance and reached for her hand. "I had to find you," he breathed.

"Why?" she asked. "Why did you need to find me, Rod?" It was almost as if she was challenging him to give her the words.

"Because I needed to tell you that I'm falling for you, honey. Before you told Nova, about us, I was going to ask you to move in with me."

"You were?" she asked. "I think that I would have liked that."

He smiled at her, "Well then, how about moving in with me?"

"That's an awfully big step, Rod," she said. "Are you sure that it's one that you're ready to make?"

"I am," he agreed. "In fact, I was going to ask you to marry me, too," he said.

Evie gasped and he pulled her into his arms. "Marry you?" she questioned.

"Yes," he whispered. "Marry me, Evie. I'm so in love with you, I can't imagine not spending the rest of our lives."

"Oh," she whispered. "I think that I'd like to marry you, too," she agreed.

"Thank God," he breathed. "I thought that I lost you, honey."

"No, I don't think that's possible, Rod. You won't ever lose me," she promised. "I think that I've been waiting for you this whole time. Every time I turned a guy down, I wondered if I'd ever find someone to give my virginity to. But then, I met you and I knew instantly—you were the one. I love you too, Rod."

He picked her up and spun her around the hallway, not caring that she was squealing and giggling, and would probably wake up everyone on the third floor. She was right—they were meant to be together. He found the woman he never knew that he was waiting for—his virgin assistant, his Evie. He had finally found her and now, he'd never let her go again.

The End

I hope you enjoyed Rodrick and Evie's story! Now, buckle up for a sneak peek at His Nerdy Assistant (Billionaire Boys Club Book 3)— coming in June from K.L. Ramsey!

LUKE

Luke Tracy wasn't sure how the hell he was going to tell his new boss and his best friend that he was going to have to take a leave of absence, but he had no choice. As the law firm's new head of security, he couldn't bring his troubles to their doorstep, but that was exactly what he was doing by just showing up to work. He wasn't sure that Alex or Rod would understand, but he had no choice but to be straight with them and let the chips fall where they may.

He decided to just bite the bullet and head upstairs to Alex's office and hope like hell that Rod was there and that Alex's cute new assistant would let him in to see both of them. He rode the elevator up to the top floor of the building and stepped off of the elevator almost running into the exact sexy assistant that he was just thinking about.

Ruby Grace was the exact opposite of his type. She was

the kind of woman that he'd usually look right past if he was out scoping women, but he wasn't. For some reason, Ruby turned him completely inside out and that wasn't going to change any time soon. Her red hair and blue eyes were a complete turn-on for him and honestly, Luke never saw himself with someone like her, not that it mattered now. He was going to have to leave town, his job, and even sexy, little Ruby behind.

"Hey, Ruby," Luke breathed, "you heading out?"

"No, just running to the restroom," she said. "Can I help you?"

"Um, sure," he said, thinking about all of the ways he'd like to ask her to help him out—most of them completely inappropriate. "I need to talk to Alex, is he in?" he asked.

"Yep," she said. "If you give me just a minute to run to the bathroom, I'll let him know that you're here," she said.

"All right," he agreed.

Alex stuck his head out of his office and smiled over at Luke. "Hey, man," he said, "come on back."

"Sorry, Mr. McTavish," Ruby apologized.

"Not a problem," Alex assured. "You take all the time you need, in fact, feel free to head home early. I have an appointment at the doctor's with Nova, so I'm going to skip out early too."

"Thank you, Mr. McTavish," Ruby said.

"Alex, Ruby," he insisted. "I told you to call me Alex." She nodded and disappeared down the hallway to the restrooms, turning back to smile at Luke as he watched her walk away.

Luke crossed the hallway and walked past Alex into his office. "Thanks for seeing me on short notice," Luke said. "I didn't mean to come up here and barge in on you."

"It's not a problem," Alex promised. "Honestly, it's a slow day. I knew that I was going to have to leave early today for my wife's OB appointment."

"Oh, yeah—I heard that Nova's pregnant, congratulations," Luke said. "Rod told me about him being an uncle again when we went out for a beer last week. Is he around today, by chance?"

"Sorry, no," Alex said. "He's been in court all day."

"I guess I can fill him in later. Listen, I need to take a leave of absence," Luke said.

"Everything all right?" Alex asked. This was the tricky part. Did he tell his new boss that he had a feeling that someone was watching him and that he was in danger, or did he come up with something that sounded a little more believable?

"I'm not sure," Luke admitted. "Last night, I found this note on my truck's windshield on my way out home." He pulled the wrinkled piece of paper out of his pocket and handed it to Alex.

"If you know what's good for you, you'll leave town now, and no one else has to die," Alex read aloud.

"Who has already died?" he asked Luke.

He shrugged, "The only person that I can think of is

my older brother, but he's been dead for almost five years now. He died in a hiking accident."

"I'm sorry to hear that, but this note makes it sound as though someone was murdered. Do you know of anyone who was murdered?" Alex asked.

"No," Luke admitted. "No one that I've known personally. I've also had a feeling like someone's been watching me for weeks now. I can't pinpoint one instance, it's just a feeling. But now, with this note, I'm starting to feel that maybe my instincts were right."

"Anything else?" Alex asked.

"Nothing tangible. I just think that it would be best for me to take some time away from the office to try to figure this all out," Luke said.

"Did you go to the authorities about this note, yet?" Alex asked.

"No," Luke admitted. "I mean, I thought that I'd be able to handle this since I am in security. I just don't want my trouble tracking me down at work. Whoever left this note had to come on company property to do so. I hate that my problems are touching your firm, Alex," he said.

"First, you need to check the security cameras to see if we got any footage of the person leaving this on your truck. Second, you're not taking a leave of absence. That's bullshit and I won't let you walk away from the firm to try to save us. If someone's coming for you, we'll figure this out together. Hell, I'll increase your security staff to help out with this issue, Luke."

"I can't ask you to do that, Alex," he insisted.

"You didn't ask, I've offered. Consider it a done deal, Luke. You're my brother's best friend. I've known you for years now, and I won't let you handle this problem alone. I say we call in the cops and give them this note as evidence," Alex said.

"Be sure about this, Alex. You have a lot of employees and I'd hate to put any of them in danger," Luke said.

"I'm sure," Alex said. "I'll help you put together a larger security team in the morning. Until then, call the cops and tell them about this note. I can't stick around. If I miss this appointment, my wife will kill me."

"No, you should go. I'll turn the note over to the authorities in the morning. I'd like some time to comb through our security footage before involving them. Maybe we'll be able to take care of this issue in-house and not have to involve them at all," Luke said.

"All right," Alex said. "Fill Rod in when you see him next, but don't spread this around the company. I don't want mass hysteria about having to come to work every day from the employees. Keep this quiet."

"Right, boss," Luke agreed. "Thanks for listening," he said.

"Any time, Luke," Alex said. "Keep me in the loop."

Luke nodded and left his office only to run into Ruby again. She had her bags and was ready to leave for the night. "Heading home?" he asked.

"I am," she agreed. He wanted to ask her who she'd be

going home to, but he knew better than to ask employees personal questions.

"You?" she asked.

"I think that I will," he said. "It's been a long day. You mind sharing an elevator?" he asked.

Ruby giggled, "Well, it does have a twelve-person capacity, so sure," she teased. What was it about Ruby that had him, so tongue-tied and saying all the wrong things?

"Right, thanks," he breathed. When the doors opened, he waited for Ruby to step in first, and then followed her on. The doors closed and she cleared her throat, watching the numbers light up over the top of the door as the elevator descended. He took the opportunity to look at Ruby, really look at her, and God, she was adorable. She wore Converse with her skirt and dressy blouse. Her red hair was pulled back in a messy bun and her thick, black glasses were falling down the bridge of her nose.

"Can you please stop looking at me like that?" she whispered, turning back to look at him.

"Looking at you?" he asked. Sure, he had been caught, but playing dumb was his only option.

"I can see you out of the corner of my eyes, Luke. You were looking at my outfit." She turned to face him, almost standing toe to toe with him. "Listen, I know that I'm odd. Heck, I've been called a nerd more times than I care to admit, but I won't let you make fun of me too."

"I wasn't going to make fun of you, Ruby," he assured.

"Then, why were you looking at me like that?" she asked.

"Because I think you're hot as hell and I was trying to memorize you right now, at this moment, until I get to see you again." Her little gasp made him rock hard. The elevator doors opened to the lobby, and he loved the way she watched him as he stepped off.

"Have a good night, Ruby," he said. She watched him until the elevator doors closed on her again and he smiled to himself. He'd finally gotten up the nerve to talk to the new girl, and as far as he was concerned, it had gone well.

RUBY

Ruby stood on the empty elevator blinking at the closed doors, trying to figure out if she had just heard Luke say what she thought that she had. He was the head of security at the firm that she worked for and every day, he checked her bags and said good morning to her, but she was sure that he did that for everyone who passed through the front doors into the building. She had no idea that he thought that she was—what did he call her? Oh yeah, hot as hell. No one had ever called her that and she was still in shock hearing the hunky hulk say those words to her.

"Wow," she breathed. "He thinks I'm hot as hell," she repeated. The words didn't even feel right on her own tongue. It was as if she was repeating a lie to herself, and she almost wanted to laugh at how ridiculous it sounded.

She was jolted backward when the elevator started to

ascend to the seventh floor. Shit, she had forgotten to get off of the damn elevator after what Luke had said to her, and now, she was going to have to work her way back down to the lobby. A part of her thought about just heading back up to her desk and hiding out there for a bit until she could sneak out of the building without running into Luke again. But that would be ridiculous. She needed to get herself together and leave the building, just as she had planned. Then, she'd go home, make herself some dinner, and open a big bottle of wine.

When the elevator stopped on the seventh floor to pick up passengers, she stepped to the back of the car and asked for someone to push the button for the lobby. If she was lucky, she'd be able to hide in the crowd of passengers who had just gotten onto the elevator and leave the building without having to see Luke again. She needed time to process everything that he had said and that was going to require copious amounts of wine.

She didn't feel as though she had taken a breath the entire time she made a run for it to her car. Ruby felt as though she was acting like a child, and if anyone knew what she was doing—running and hiding from a grown man, they'd believe she was a complete fool. How many women would run away from a man who looked like Luke Tracy? She was betting that the answer was not many.

As soon as she made it home to her tiny apartment that she had rented purely because it was close to the office, she pulled off her jacket and Converse and practically flung herself onto the sofa. What a day and all she could hear in her head was Luke's voice telling her that he thought that she was hot as hell. It was playing on a loop up there and nothing she did would shake it loose.

The knock at her front door startled her from her daydreams and she sighed, standing to answer it. She pulled the door open and found her neighbor, Millie standing on the other side.

"Hey," Millie said.

"Hi, Millie," Ruby breathed. "Listen I just got home and I'm exhausted."

"Oh," Millie whispered. "So, you're not up for dinner then. It's fine, really. We can just reschedule."

"Reschedule?" Ruby asked. "Crap, I forgot about our dinner plans," she said. "I'm so sorry. Come on in." she stood aside to let her friend in, and Millie looked hesitant.

"It's fine if you want to reschedule," Millie said again.

"Not at all," Ruby insisted. "I was about to open a bottle of wine to help me unwind. I'm sure I'll get my second wind as soon as I down my first glass. We can order some takeout if that works for you."

"Well, I could go for some Asian takeout," Millie agreed.

"Deal," Ruby said. "I'll call in our order and you grab the wine from the fridge and open it. You know where everything is."

"Yep," Millie said, seeming to pep up a bit. Millie had

been her only friend in town since she moved into the apartment two months ago. Honestly, besides a few people at work, she didn't know anyone in her new hometown. Being alone usually worked for her since she was kind of a homebody and very much a loner. Ruby didn't go out to clubs or parties like other girls her age. At only twenty-four, she should have been living it up, going on dates with men her age, but she was always a bit shy and tried to hide away. It was easy to do since guys weren't beating down her door, begging her to go out with them. No one wanted to date a nerd.

Millie poured her a glass of wine and handed it to her. "So, how's the new job?" She asked Ruby that every time they got together. She had been working for Alex McTavish for almost two months now, and Ruby always gave her the same answer.

"It's great," she said. "Although something interesting happened today."

"Share," Millie insisted. Ruby instantly regretted bringing up the incident with Luke. She and Millie weren't friends like that yet, but Ruby had no one else to spill the beans to.

"The hot guy in charge of security at my building told me that I was hot. Well, he said, 'hot as hell,' but you get the gist."

"Oh—that is something," Millie agreed. "Do you like this guy?"

"I mean, I never really thought about him that way.

Sure, I've noticed him and all, but I never thought that he even knew who I was," Ruby admitted.

"But he does, so you like him?" Millie pushed.

"We've only said a handful of words to each other, but yeah, I think he's nice," Ruby admitted.

"And hot," Millie said. "Don't forget that you said that he's hot."

"Yes," Ruby agreed. "He's nice and hot." God, she sounded like an idiot and now, she fully regretted bringing up the subject with Millie. "Let me call in the order. You want your normal meal?"

"Yep," Millie agreed. "P7—the orange chicken and fried rice combo."

Ruby nodded and told the woman who answered the call their order. She was promised that the food would get to them in about twenty minutes, and she wondered how she'd be able to change the subject because talking about hot, nice Luke until their food got there wasn't going to happen.

She ended the call and Millie sat down on the sofa next to her, wearing a huge smile. "So, what are you going to do about Luke?" she asked.

"Um, nothing," Ruby admitted. "I work with him, and I'd be mortified if I asked him out and he said no."

"I get that," Millie said. "I've been turned down before and it hurts. It doesn't hurt to play things safe," she said. "Let him come to you." As if that would ever happen. Guys like Luke didn't come for her—ever.

Ruby did her best to make small talk while Millie kept trying to drive the topic back to Luke. Ruby said a little prayer of thanks when the delivery guy knocked on her front door.

"That must be the food," she said. "Give me just a minute." She pulled the front door open and gasped when she found Luke standing there. "You're not the delivery guy," she said.

"Who is it?" Millie asked. She joined Ruby in the doorway and gasped a bit as she looked Luke over. "Wow, the delivery guy's hot."

"Millie, this is Luke," she said.

"You weren't kidding, he is hot," Millie said.

"You told her about me?" Luke asked, smiling at her like a loon. Ruby suddenly wondered how the hell she had gotten herself into this mess. The better question was how the hell was she going to get out of it?

"No," she lied.

"Oh, she told me all about how you told her she's hot while you both were on the elevator," Millie shared.

Ruby shot Millie a look, trying to silently tell her to shut up, and Luke laughed. "What can I do for you, Luke?" she asked.

"I'm in a bit of trouble and I need your help," he admitted.

"How can I help you?" Ruby asked.

"By giving me a place to lay low," he said. "I'll explain everything, if you'll just let me in, Ruby, please."

"How about you send my order over to me and I'll leave you two alone," Millie asked.

"You don't have to leave, Millie," Ruby insisted.

"I don't mind," she said. "What are friends for?" She winked at Ruby and all she could muster was rolling her eyes.

"Fine," she said. "I'll have the delivery guy bring your half over when he gets here," Ruby agreed.

"Nice meeting you, Luke," Millie said as she brushed a little too closely by the big guy. He nodded and gave her his best smile, but Ruby could see that it didn't reach his eyes.

Ruby let Luke into her place and shut her front door. She didn't even offer the poor guy something to drink before she crossed her arms over her chest and told him to, "Spill it."

"I think I'm being watched," he admitted, "and, I need a place to stay for a while. I had no one else to turn to," he said.

"You have no other friends or family in the area?" she asked. Sure, she was prying, but she couldn't help it.

"No," he admitted. "Well, no friends that I want involved in this mess. Alex and Rod both have families and I'm worried that whoever is watching me is really trying to get to them."

"To the McTavish's?" she asked. "Why would someone want to hurt them?"

"I'm not sure, but I need time and space to figure that all out. That's where you come in, Ruby."

"Fine," he said. "You can hang out here for as long as you'd like. But for the record, you don't need to lie to me and tell me that I'm hot next time you want something from me."

He dropped his duffel bag in the corner of her small family room and turned back to smile at her. "For the record, honey," he said, giving her back her words, "it wasn't a lie."

His Nerdy Assistant (Billionaire Boys Club Book 3)—coming June 14, 2022, from K.L. Ramsey! Universal Link->

What's coming up next from K.L. Ramsey? No Limits (Dirty Desires Book 3) is coming May 16, 2022, and you won't want to miss it! You'll also get the bonus novella, Hard Limits, with this book!

LINCOLN

Lincoln West pushed the button to call his private elevator back up to his penthouse. He was late for the meeting with his new security firm and if this morning's events were any indication, he needed all the help he could get securing his home.

The break-in wasn't just unexpected it was deemed downright impossible by his current—well, former security firm. As soon as the cops showed up to take his statement he called his office and got the name of the security firm his business partner, Ethan Jacobs, used for his home. They were targets and it wasn't a matter of if someone else would break back into his penthouse but when. Ethan set up the meeting with Blue Security Firm at their office and promised to meet him there.

Ethan was his rock and Linc wasn't sure what he would

do without the guy. Besides being his business partner, Ethan was his best friend but if he was being completely truthful, Linc wanted so much more with him. That was something he had always kept to himself though, too afraid to tell Ethan his feelings only to be rejected and lose everything.

Ethan was waiting for Linc in the parking garage when he pulled in. He parked his Mercedes G class next to Ethan's Audi S8 and smirked over at his friend. They had many heated debates over who had the better ride. The difference was, Linc usually opted to drive himself while Ethan had to have his pampered ass driven around by a chauffeur. Linc jumped out of his SUV and slammed his door shut, making sure he locked the car up behind him. He wouldn't be taking any chances now that he came face to face with the barrel of a gun. When you stare down your mortality, your whole perspective changes.

"No driver tonight? You roughing it, Ethan?" Linc teased. His best friend laughed and pulled him in for a quick side hug.

"I didn't think I'd need a driver but then your weak ass security measures failed and well, here we are," Ethan teased. "You good man?" he asked. Linc wanted to tell him that he wasn't good. That waking up in the middle of the night to find someone standing over his fucking bed with a gun pointed at his head wasn't his idea of good. Ethan must have seen his answer in his expression and he frowned. "That bad?" he asked.

"Yeah," Linc breathed. "I'll tell you about it when we get inside. It's not a story I want to tell more than I have to. Thanks for meeting me here, man, and for setting up this meeting." Ethan wrapped his arm around Linc's shoulder and gave him a playful shake.

"That's what best friends are for, Linc. You call me and I make arrangements. Besides, I think you're going to like Ella," Ethan said. His best friend was always trying to fix him up with women and men, for that matter. Ethan knew that Linc was bisexual and he never made Linc feel that he couldn't be himself around him.

"Ella?" Linc questioned. Although he had a sneaky feeling he wasn't going to like Ethan's answer. "Who's Ella?"

"She's the head of the new security firm you're about to hire," Ethan said. He held the elevator door for Linc to get in and for just a minute, he thought about running the fuck out of there because this whole thing felt like a setup. Ethan chuckled and slapped Linc on the back. "Just keep an open mind man—she owns one of the top security firms in Atlanta and you'll be lucky if she takes you on."

"Wait—I thought you said she outfitted your security at your place," Linc said. Ethan pushed the button to take them to the top floor of the building where their offices were located.

"I did," Ethan said, not giving much more detail.

"Shit, Ethan," Linc grumbled. "Tell me you didn't sleep with her already."

"No, not that she hasn't tried to get into my pants. I haven't slept with her yet—I thought we could make her an offer she won't be able to pass up—two for the price of one." Linc looked over at his friend and Ethan pretended to be interested in the passing numbers that flashed across the top of the elevator doors as they climbed to the top floor.

"Two for the price of one—what the hell does that mean?" Linc asked. The elevator doors opened and Ethan stepped out looking back over his shoulder to where Linc stood frozen in place.

"It means just what you think it does, Linc. Time to stop pretending and take what we both want, Babe."

ELLA

Ella watched as sexy Ethan Jacobs stepped free from the private elevator that brought him up to his top-floor office. She had known Ethan for years and apparently, only the best would suffice for him. It was one of the reasons she was called to West Investments—she was the best. Ella was just hoping that Ethan was finally going to give her the chance to prove that she was good at more than just security. God, the man was walking sin in a suit and all she could think about was how good he probably looked underneath it. His tailor-made suits left nothing to the imagination with the way they hugged his bulging muscles and other bulges a lady didn't talk about. But, Ella wasn't a lady—not by any stretch of the imagination.

Ethan smiled and met her halfway across the big conference room she was asked to wait in. He reached out to take her hand into his and God, she felt the caress of his touch down in her core. What was it about this man that made her want to do sinfully wicked things on his conference room table—glass walls be damned?

"So good to see you again, Ella," he said looking her body up and down. Ella was damn happy that she had taken the time to fix her hair and make-up before meeting with Ethan—even opting for her sexy black heels that made her feel every inch of confidence she now exuded. Yeah, Ethan was checking her out and she was fine with it. She welcomed his attention since she had been trying to get it for so long now.

"You too, Ethan," she purred. "Although I'm not thrilled about the hour, I'm happy to take a meeting with you."

"Yeah—sorry about the three in the morning wake-up call, but I need your help." Ethan's business partner, Lincoln West, joined them and the conference room and Ella suddenly felt way too hot. She had never met the guy but his sexy smile and sun-kissed skin made his blue eyes look even bluer than the picture she had seen plastered all over the front pages of the local gossip magazines. He was listed as one of Atlanta's most eligible bachelors and she could see the appeal. Number five on the list of men with money and looks in the area was still holding her hand in his and staring her down as if waiting for her to swallow her damn tongue.

"Ella, this is Lincoln West, my business partner," Ethan introduced them.

"Pleasure to meet you, Mr. West," Ella said, suddenly very aware of how nervous she sounded.

"Pleasure is all mine, Ella. Please, call me Linc," he offered. Ella nodded and released his hand.

"What can I do for you gentlemen?" she asked getting right down to business. It was what she was good at and right now, she needed a distraction from the two sexy alphas who were crowding her personal space.

"My penthouse was broken into and I need my security overhauled. Ethan says your firm is one of the best in Atlanta," Linc said.

Ella shot Ethan a smile, "The best, actually," she challenged. Ethan threw back his head and laughed and she was sure it was the sexiest thing she'd ever witnessed. His dark hair fell over one eye and she imagined that was how Ethan would look when he came—but that wasn't why she was there and thinking about Linc or Ethan coming wasn't going to land her the job.

"How soon can you start?" Linc asked. He stared her down like she was going to be his next meal and Ella wasn't sure if she should run and hide or throw herself at the blond god.

"Um, I'd have to check with my assistant but I'm sure we can squeeze you in soon," she promised.

"I'd appreciate that, Ella," he said. "Thank you for taking the time to come out in the middle of the night."

"Of course," Ella said, feeling a bit dismissed. "If that will be all, I'll show myself out," she offered.

"Wait," Ethan growled. "One more thing before you go."

ETHAN

Ethan liked the fact that he could throw Ella Blue off her game. Hell, he had made both Linc and Ella a little flustered tonight and he had to admit—he liked it. Ella was sexy as fuck and she wore those heels that she always did—the ones that looked like she'd break her neck walking in them but God, he wanted them wrapped around his neck, digging into his back while he ate her pussy. Yeah—Ella Blue was his walking wet dream and there would be no way he'd let her walk out of that conference room without tasting her first. From the look on Linc's handsome face, he'd be on board with Ethan's plan.

Ella stood in front of him, and he could tell that she was anticipating his next command. She'd be a perfect submissive, even with her dominant businesswoman persona. Ella was just begging him to tell her what to do next and that made him hard.

"Yes, Ethan," she breathlessly purred. Yeah, she was just as turned on as he was but the real question was would Linc be on board.

"Can you give Linc and me just a moment?" he asked. Ethan didn't miss the flash of disappointment in her eyes. Ella seemed to be hoping for him to say something else but he'd get to that. "Linc—can I talk to you in the hallway, man?" he asked. His best friend looked at him like he had lost his mind and hell, maybe he had. What he was about to do would cross all the damn lines but he didn't give a fuck. Ethan was done with hiding who he was and what he wanted. He wanted Linc and hiding his feelings wasn't how he wanted to play things anymore.

Linc followed him out into the small corridor that led back to their offices and Ethan used the element of surprise and pushed him up against the wall, causing a loud thunk he was sure Ella would be able to hear. "What the fuck, Ethan?" Linc growled.

"I'm done pretending that there's nothing between the two of us, Linc," Ethan whispered. His lips were so close to Linc's he could almost taste him. "Tell me you don't want this," Ethan ordered. Linc looked into his eyes and for just a minute, he thought he was going to deny him. Ethan wasn't a fool—he could see the way Linc checked him out when he thought he wasn't paying attention but he didn't ever let things go further than just harmless flirtation.

"I want this," Linc sighed. "I have for a long time now." Ethan leaned in to kiss Linc and hesitated, looking into his eyes for confirmation that he was on board for what Ethan wanted next. Linc gave a curt nod and Ethan pressed his mouth against Linc's demanding that he open for him. When Linc didn't comply, Ethan reached down to cup his friend's balls, causing him to moan into his mouth, granting his tongue access. Linc thrust into Ethan's hand and God, it took every ounce of his restraint not to fuck him right there in that hallway with Ella waiting for them in the next room.

"Fuck," Ella whispered. "That's hot," she said. Ethan broke their kiss, leaving both him and Linc breathless, and smiled at Ella who had poked her head out of the conference room to spy on them.

"You were watching us?" he challenged.

"Yeah," she breathed. "I heard a banging on the wall and thought something happened. I didn't mean to stick my nose where it didn't belong. I'll just leave and let you two—"

"No," Linc and Ethan said in unison. "Stay," Ethan demanded.

"Listen," Ella came out into the hallway to stand in front of them and Ethan loved the way she didn't back down or cower at the way the two of them towered over her. "I don't want to get in the middle of whatever you two have going on," she insisted.

Linc reached down and took her hand into his own and

Ethan did the same with her other hand. "What if we want you to be in the middle of whatever this is?" Ethan asked.

"Wait—" Ella stuttered, "I thought you called me here to handle Linc's security breach," she asked.

"I did," Ethan said. "But, I think you might be up for handling a few other things, too," he challenged. The one thing Ethan knew for sure about Ella Blue was that she didn't ever back down from a challenge. He and Linc crowded her and she turned the cutest shade of pink. Ethan was sure that wasn't something that Ella Blue did very easily—show vulnerability but he liked that side of her. She seemed softer and Lord help him—even sexier.

"I think she needs us to spell it out for her, man," Linc said. "We want to put you in the middle, Honey—between Ethan and me. You up for that?" Leave it to Linc to just lay it all out but that was the way his friend worked. It was one of the things he loved most about his business partner.

Ella didn't hesitate. She even seemed to stand a little taller in her sexy ass heels and Ethan knew that she was thinking of Linc's request as a challenge. "I'm game," she said. "Just say when and where."

Linc nodded and picked her up, throwing her over his shoulder in a fireman's hold. "How about here and now?" he said, carrying her back to his corner office. Ethan trailed them and when the sexy vixen looked up at him as if pleading for help, he just shrugged. There would be no stopping his best friend. Once Linc set his mind to doing something, there would be no stopping him. And from the way he had his hand possessively on Ella's curvy ass, he wanted to "do" her.

No Limits (Dirty Desires Book 3) Universal Link-> https://books2read.com/u/4El9ee

ABOUT K.L. RAMSEY & BE KELLY

Romance Rebel fighting for Happily Ever After!

K. L. Ramsey currently resides in West Virginia (Go Mountaineers!). In her spare time, she likes to read romance novels, go to WVU football games and attend book club (aka-drink wine) with girlfriends. K. L. enjoys writing Contemporary Romance, Erotic Romance, and Sexy Ménage! She loves to write strong, capable women and bossy, hot as hell alphas, who fall ass over tea kettle for them. And of course, her stories always have a happy ending. But wait—there's more!

Somewhere along the writing path, K.L. developed a love of ALL things paranormal (but has a special affinity for shifters <YUM!!>)!! She decided to take a chance and create another persona- BE Kelly- to bring you all of her yummy shifters, seers, and everything paranormal (plus a hefty dash of MC!).

K. L. RAMSEY'S SOCIAL MEDIA

Ramsey's Rebels - K.L. Ramsey's Readers Group
https://www.facebook.com/groups/ramseysrebels

KL Ramsey & BE Kelly's ARC Team
https://www.facebook.com/groups/klramseyandbekellyarcteam

KL Ramsey and BE Kelly's Newsletter
https://mailchi.mp/4e73ed1b04b9/authorklramsey/

KL Ramsey and BE Kelly's Website
https://www.klramsey.com

- facebook.com/kl.ramsey.58
- instagram.com/itsprivate2
- bookbub.com/profile/k-l-ramsey
- twitter.com/KLRamsey5
- amazon.com/K.L.-Ramsey/e/B0799P6JGJ

BE KELLY'S SOCIAL MEDIA

BE Kelly's Reader's group
https://www.facebook.com/groups/kellsangelsreadersgroup/

- facebook.com/be.kelly.564
- instagram.com/bekellyparanormalromanceauthor
- twitter.com/BEKelly9
- bookbub.com/profile/be-kelly
- amazon.com/BE-Kelly/e/B081LLD38M

WORKS BY K. L. RAMSEY

The Relinquished Series Box Set

Love Times Infinity

Love's Patient Journey

Love's Design

Love's Promise

Harvest Ridge Series Box Set

Worth the Wait

The Christmas Wedding

Line of Fire

Torn Devotion

Fighting for Justice

Last First Kiss Series Box Set

Theirs to Keep

Theirs to Love

Theirs to Have

Theirs to Take

Second Chance Summer Series

True North

The Wrong Mister Right

Ties That Bind Series

Saving Valentine

Blurred Lines

Dirty Little Secrets

Ties That Bind Box Set

Taken Series

Double Bossed

Double Crossed

Double The Mistletoe

Double Down

Owned

His Secret Submissive

His Reluctant Submissive

His Cougar Submissive

His Nerdy Submissive

His Stubborn Submissive- Coming soon!

Alphas in Uniform

Hellfire

Royal Bastards MC

Savage Heat

Whiskey Tango

Can't Fix Cupid

Ratchet's Revenge

Patched for Christmas

Love at First Fight

Dizzy's Desire

Savage Hell MC Series

Roadkill

REPOssession

Dirty Ryder

Hart's Desire

Axel's Grind

Razor's Edge

Lone Star Rangers

Don't Mess With Texas

Sweet Adeline

Dash of Regret

Austin's Starlet

Ranger's Revenge

Smokey Bandits MC Series

Aces Wild

Queen of Hearts

Full House

King of Clubs

Joker's Wild

Tirana Brothers (Social Rejects Syndicate

Llir

Altin

Veton

Dirty Desire Series

Torrid

Clean Sweep

Mountain Men Mercenary Series

Eagle Eye

Hacker

Widowmaker

Deadly Sins Syndicate (Mafia Series)

Pride

Envy

Greed

Lust

Wrath- Coming soon!

Sloth- Coming soon!

Gluttony- Coming soon!

Forgiven Series

Confession of a Sinner

Confessions of a Saint

Confessions of a Rebel- Coming soon!

Chasing Serendipity Series

Kismet

Sealed With a Kiss Series

Kissable

Garo Syndicate Trilogy

Edon

Bekim

Rovena- Coming soon!

Billionaire Boys Club

His Naughty Assistant

His Virgin Assistant

His Nerdy Assistant

His Curvy Assistant

His Bossy Assistant

His Rebellious Assistant

Grumpy Mountain Men Series

Grizz

The Bridezilla Series

Happily Ever After- Almost

Rope 'Em and Ride 'Em Series

Saddle Up- Coming soon!

Craving the Cowboy- Coming soon!

WORKS BY BE KELLY (K.L.'S ALTER EGO...)

Reckoning MC Seer Series

Reaper

Tank

Raven

Reckoning MC Series Box Set

Perdition MC Shifter Series

Ringer

Rios

Trace

Perdition 3 Book Box Set

Wren's Pack- Coming soon!

Silver Wolf Shifter Series

Daddy Wolf's Little Seer

Daddy Wolf's Little Captive

Daddy Wolf's Little Star

Rogue Enforcers

Juno

Blaze- Coming soon

Elite Enforcers

A Very Rogue Christmas Novella

One Rogue Turn

Graystone Academy Series

Eden's Playground

Violet's Surrender- Coming soon!

Holly's Hope (A Christmas Novella)- Coming soon!

Renegades Shifter Series

Pandora's Promise

Kinsley's Pact

Leader of the Pack Series

Wren's Pack

Made in United States
Orlando, FL
17 March 2024